MADE TO HOLD YOU

DECADES: A JOURNEY OF AFRICAN AMERICAN ROMANCE (BOOK 9)

ELLE WRIGHT

MADE TO HOLD YOU

Decades: A Journey of African American Romance
Book 9

Elle Wright

Made To Hold You
Copyright @ 2018 by Elle Wright
Paperback ISBN: 978-0-9994213-1-4

Excerpt from *Beyond Forever*
copyright @ 2017 by Elle Wright
Excerpt from *Touched By You*
copyright @ 2018 by Elle Wright

Elle Wrights Books, LLC
Ypsilanti, Michigan
www.ElleWright.com

Editor:
LaToya C. Smith, LCS Literary Services

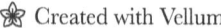 Created with Vellum

Layla Johnson had a picture perfect life: a career as an educator, a beautiful daughter, a son on the way, and a loving husband. Only Layla didn't count on the effect the burgeoning war on drugs would have on her family and her world. And on one rainy night, everything that she worked to attain is destroyed. Now, she's on her own, with two young children, a mounting pile of debt…and the past knocking at her door.

Lincoln Wilson broke the one thing he treasured most. Instead of spending the rest of his life doting on his beautiful wife and children, he's alone, haunted by his many mistakes. Determined to make amends, Lincoln works to put the pieces of his life back together again. And although it's an uphill battle, he is up for the challenge. The last step in Lincoln's program is to prove to his wife that he can be the man she needs. When he shows up on her doorstep ready to reclaim his life, will Layla let him in?

To my parents, Leon and Regina. I love you. Mom, you are missed.

ACKNOWLEDGMENTS

First and foremost, I want to thank God. He is everything I need. He makes my life complete.

To my husband and children, thanks for being my calm in the storm. I wouldn't be me without you.

To my father, you are The Phoenix. Despite the challenges you've faced, you have risen from the ashes. You're my daddy, my friend. And I'll always be your "girly-girl."

To Wayne Jordan, thank you for this opportunity.

To my editor and friend, LaToya C. Smith, thank you for pushing me to improve. You've been a Godsend.

A special shout-out to the amazing readers and awesome writers that I've met on this journey. There would be no "Elle Wright" without your love and encouragement, your enthusiasm and understanding.

PROLOGUE

April 1987

Just say no.

Layla Johnson gripped the wooden bat in her hand and swallowed past the lump in her throat. As she stared at the townhome with the green door in front of her, she wondered how her life had taken such a drastic turn. Scanning the area, she watched strange people stagger out of the house, listened to the men and women milling around outside.

To an outsider, Prospect Woods might seem like a nice, quiet neighborhood—one of several in her hometown of Ypsilanti, Michigan. But to locals, it was anything but. Once the sun set, the apartment community turned into a den of thieves, prostitutes, and junkies. Layla never thought she'd have a reason to step foot inside the gate until she'd received a call from an anonymous caller telling her that she could find her husband, Lincoln, there.

Layla sucked in a deep breath, smoothing a hand over her stomach. In a few weeks, her son would arrive. But in a few minutes, her life would change forever. Over the past year all of her dreams, all of their plans, had gone up in smoke. Literally. Because the man that she'd promised to love forever had hurt her to her core. And because the love of her life had let his addiction destroy what they had spent years building. Gone were the hopes of a good life with her small family of four. The warmth of a love that seemed to shine so bright had turned to a bitter cold.

Layla had struggled with whether her marriage was worth saving. And every time she'd warred with herself, she'd ultimately decide it was—until a few days ago. Her husband, Lincoln, had been a no-show when she'd been rushed to the hospital with early labor pains. She'd cried for Linc as the doctors had rushed to her aid, as they attempted to stop her labor. But he didn't come, he didn't call. Fortunately, the doctors were able to stop the contractions, and she'd been released from the hospital with strict instructions to stay in the bed and avoid stress.

Walking into her empty home after her short hospital stay had hurt Layla, but she'd held it together. Realizing that Linc had taken her wedding ring and all of the money she'd hidden away for her maternity leave had gutted her. He'd made his decision. The drugs were obviously more important than her, than their children. The hard decision to walk away from her husband was devastating, but necessary. She had two innocent children to think about. Tomorrow, she would start a new life without Lincoln, but tonight she had to make sure he was safe. Once she did that, she'd make her move.

Layla felt tears well in her eyes, and willed them not to fall. Her hands trembled as she gripped the bat. She had no idea what she would find behind those doors. Was Linc still there? Was he still alive? Was he alone? So many questions ran through her mind on an endless loop. But now wasn't the time to get emotional. She had to get the job done. Letting out a slow breath, she gripped the wood tighter.

"It's okay, baby." Linc's mother, Martha, squeezed Layla's hand, offering strong support.

When Layla had received the anonymous call, the older woman was the first person she'd thought to call. Martha had been so supportive, had loved her like she was her own child. That's what the Wilson clan did. Once you were one of them, you remained one of them.

"I'm scared, Ma."

Ma offered her a small smile, but Layla knew it wasn't genuine. After all, there was nothing to smile about. Layla wasn't the only one hurting. Ma had suffered unimaginable loss as well. They all had. "I am, too. But when you came to me, I told you I could handle this on my own."

Layla shook her head. There was no way she could let Ma do this without her. The woman standing before her had done more for Layla in the few years she'd known her than some of her own family members.

When she'd met Martha, the older woman took one look at her and told her to "sit her butt down and stay a while." From that moment on, the two women had bonded. Martha had taught Layla how to make gravy, showed her how to plant tomatoes, and held her when her own mother died from breast cancer. Martha definitely had a stake in this.

"Come on," Martha said. "We have to do this, baby."

"I know. Let's go." The night breeze whipped across Layla's cheek. It was way past her bedtime, especially on a school night. Her students would definitely call her on it if she didn't give them her all tomorrow. Peering down at her stomach, she couldn't help the small smile that always accompanied a kick. Being pregnant was a blessing, being a mother was everything to her. "It's going to be okay, son. Mama's going to always take care of you."

They hurried to the door, Layla following close behind Martha. As they approached the green door of the townhouse, she once again wondered what she would actually find on the other side. After all, they were getting ready to enter a known, and very active, drug house. Would her heart be able to take it?

Music blared inside the small home, and Layla could hear the muffled sound of voices, laughter. According to the woman who'd called her, the party had been in full swing for hours, with people coming in and out. The smell of smoke seeped through the open window to the side.

Martha nudged Layla with her elbow. "Ready?"

Layla set the bat down for a minute to wipe her sweaty palms, then lifted it up high. "When you are."

The glint of silver in Martha's hand caught Layla's eye. Her mother-in-law never went anywhere without her "piece." The small .38 special stayed in her purse or under her mattress. Layla watched as Martha checked the barrel once more. Then, without another word, Martha kicked in the door.

It was chaos as women screamed and people pushed past her and out the door. Layla's trembling hands held on to the bat for dear life, all while trying to stay upright.

"Where is my son?" Martha demanded, to no one in particular.

Layla scanned the immediate area, locking eyes with the remaining people. The room was trashed, cups on the floor, cigarette butts everywhere. And the smell...it was toxic. She felt bile in her throat rise and before she could stop herself, she threw up on the floor. Ma was behind her, rubbing her back and whispering nonsensical words to her. It took several moments to regain her composure, but she finally stood to her full height and shot Ma a glance.

"I'm sorry," Layla whispered. "I'm okay."

Before last year, Layla had been blissfully ignorant to all the telltale signs of drug abuse. She'd never had to deal with anything remotely like it in her childhood. She'd grown up in the church, spent most of her days in the four walls of her family's place of worship. It wasn't until college that she'd been introduced to alcohol, cigarettes, and men. One man, in particular. The man she thought she'd love forever.

"Don't make me repeat myself," Martha growled, snapping Layla out of her thoughts.

A skinny man shuffled toward them and Layla immediately recognized him. Lincoln's best friend, Rod. Layla had never liked him because she instinctively knew he was trouble. He'd always showed up at inappropriate hours, looking worse for the wear. When she'd met him several years ago, he'd been a healthy, stocky man. Now, he looked thin, frail, and haggard.

He eyed her, before turning to Martha. "He's in the back." He pointed toward a door. "But you shouldn't go back there."

Rod was talking to her now, not Martha. Layla's chin trembled. "Why?"

"You don't want to go back there," he said, a solemn look in his eyes.

Martha grumbled a curse, and waived her gun toward him. "Rod, get the hell out of here before I tell your wife where you been."

When Rod scurried out of the door, Layla told Martha, "I'll go."

"You sure?"

"Yes."

Layla walked to the closed door, stepping over broken glass and scattered pieces of foil. Sighing, she pushed it open. Passed on out the floor, in a pool of vomit, was her husband.

"Oh no." She dropped her bat and hurried over to him, kneeling down before him. "Lincoln?" She turned him over and shook him. "Get up."

There was no movement, no sign of life. She picked up his wrist and placed two fingers between the bone and the tendon over his radial artery, like she'd been taught to do in the required first aid certification class she'd taken every year since she'd become a teacher. When she finally felt his pulse, she slumped over as relief coursed through her.

She slapped both of his cheeks, and shook him again. "Linc, wake up. Come on, baby. Get up. Please."

Layla startled when she heard movement in the corner of the room. "Who's there?" She'd been so focused on Linc, she hadn't stopped to see if anyone was in the room with him. "Come out, whoever you are."

A man, dressed in a dirty, wrinkled suit crawled out from behind the long, heavy curtains. Layla eyed her discarded bat near the door and considered going for it, but the man didn't seem to know where he was. He had a dazed look in his eyes and a shaky gait as his stood to his feet and walked toward her. She hugged Linc to her and met the man's gaze.

"What do you want?" she asked.

The man's eyes softened. "You should go home. He's hopeless. Just like I am." Without another word, the man shuffled out of the room.

Layla peered down at Linc. She traced the lines of his forehead and the arch of his nose. "Please, Linc. Wake up." She hit him again, and shook him one last time. "Damn-it, wake up!"

Finally, his eyes cracked open. "LaLa," he breathed. "You're here."

His nickname for her, LaLa, used to make her feel so special, so loved. Today, though, it gutted her. "I'm here. Come on, get up."

It took an hour to get him out of the house and settled at Ma's home. She'd bathed him and tucked him in before leaving the spare bedroom.

Martha held out a mug of hot tea when Layla walked into the kitchen, but she declined the offering. "No, thanks, Ma. I'd better go."

"Baby, don't do this. He can get better. We can make sure he does."

The tears that had threatened to fall all night finally fell. Shaking her head, she said, "I can't. I have to do what's best for my kids. You know that."

Martha dabbed her own eyes with a paper towel. "I do." She hugged Layla. "I love you, baby."

Layla rested her chin on Martha's shoulder. "I love you, too, Ma. And I love him, as well. But I can't do this anymore."

Martha pulled back and brushed her hand over Layla's cheek. "I understand. You go home, now. Rest. I'll check in on you in the morning."

Layla nodded. "Thanks."

Slowly, Layla made her way to the door. It took everything in her not to go back, to climb in the bed with Lincoln. But she'd made up her mind. It was over.

Turning back to Martha, Layla said, "And please—"

"Layla, I'll keep him away. For now. Until he's better."

"It's for the best," Layla said. "I don't want my kids to be around him when he's like this."

Then, Layla walked out of the house, away from him, and away from their life.

7

ONE

One year later

"I don't get it, Layla."

Sighing, Layla picked up a stuffed animal off the floor and tossed it into the playpen. "What don't you get?" She straightened up the magazines on the table, before turning to Martha.

The puzzled look on her mother-in-law's—well, ex mother-in-law—face told her this wasn't going to be an easy conversation. In Martha's arms, Layla's son slept peacefully.

"I don't see why you had to change your name back to Johnson."

Layla shrugged. "Because the divorce is final. I'm not married to Linc anymore."

"Still, many women get divorced and keep their married names. Look at me, shit."

"Shh." Layla craned her head to check on her four-year-old daughter, Courtney, who was happily playing with her baby doll on the family room floor. "You know she picks up every little thing we say. I don't want her running around saying 'shit' repeatedly at preschool."

Martha waved a dismissive hand toward her. "Chile, that baby isn't paying me any attention."

"Please, Ma. Today is supposed to be a happy day. Can we not talk about this?"

Layla had been planning her son's first birthday party for weeks. It wasn't a big party, but she wanted it to be perfect nonetheless. She held her arms out. "Do you want me to take him?"

Martha nuzzled her grandson's nose, and he made a cute little noise. "He's fine right here. I barely get to see my beautiful grandkids as it is."

Guilt surged through Layla at Martha's remark. Since that fateful night a little over a year ago, she'd distanced herself from several members of his family. Not because she didn't love them, but because she blamed them. It was no secret that a few extended family members had introduced Linc to drugs. Logically, she knew Linc was a grown man and capable of saying no, but it still burned to know that the same people who pretended to love him would let him drown in his addiction.

Unfortunately, in her attempt to get far away from the pain, she'd limited visits with Martha. She would never keep the children away from the woman who was like a second mother to her, but Martha was rarely alone. The older woman always had a house full of people, and Layla didn't want to run into anyone that would put her in a bad head space.

"I'm sorry, Ma. But you know how I feel about…" Layla didn't want to come right out and name names, even though she suspected Martha already knew who the culprits were. Yes, the Wilsons were a huge family, but one rarely got anything over on Martha.

"Layla, now you know I would never let anyone do anything to my grandchildren."

"I know," Layla assured Martha, joining her at the table finally. She squeezed Martha's hand. "It's just hard. And I've been so busy working and taking care of the kids, I'm just tired when I get off."

Martha smiled sadly. "I understand, baby. You forget, I've been there. That ole husband of mine never changed a single diaper or cooked a meal that didn't consist of cold bologna on white bread. I know what it's like to work so hard during the day and then come home and work in the evening. But what I'm trying to tell you is you don't have to do this alone."

Here we go again. "Ma, Linc and I are divorced. We're not getting back together."

"But you two made vows to stay together through good and bad times."

"He broke those vows in so many ways. You know, I know what people say about me when they think I don't hear them. I see the looks from his friends and your family. Everyone thinks I should have stayed, that I should have stood by him with a smile on my face all in the name of family. No one seems to care about what I went through trying to hold my family together by myself."

"I don't think that's true."

Layla snorted. "Ma, you tell me every chance you get that you believe we'll get back together."

"And you tell me every chance you get that it's not going to happen," Martha argued. "Listen, I'm the last person to tell anyone how to live. But I do know a few things about life. What did I always tell you? Two heads are better than one any day... Even if one is a goat head."

Layla couldn't stop the laughter that burst out of her

mouth at one of Martha's famous sayings. "I still don't understand that one, Ma."

Martha reached out and cupped Layla's chin. "Linc has struggled, but he's still a good man. I believe he can be the man he once was, but he needs his family."

Layla knew that a sober Lincoln would do anything to protect his family. But she couldn't count on Linc to remain drug-free. "I needed him, too, Ma. I needed him with me when I went into early labor with Lil Linc. I could've had his son early, but he wasn't there. Anything could have gone wrong and he wouldn't have been present."

"He loves you, Layla. He cares about you and the kids."

"He didn't care about us when he was out there in the streets. He didn't care about me when he stole my money to get a fix. Ma, he pawned my wedding ring for drugs. He didn't care that I had to rob Peter to pay Paul just to keep the lights on. My central air is out of commission, the fireplace is leaking. This house is falling apart. How am I supposed to believe that he cares?"

Her daily frustration of living this life without her partner bubbled to the surface. Linc had made promises. He swore before God and the church and his entire family that he would honor her all the days of their lives. But he didn't. And she was still picking up the pieces.

"It wasn't him, Layla. It was those drugs. They take good people and turn them inside out. I know first-hand. He's my son. I love him, and I know you love him, too."

"I do love him, but what does that have to do with anything? I still have bills to pay, I still have to work every day to fix the mess he created. I've already lost enough. I'm getting through by the grace of God, but I can't put myself back into an impossible situation."

"Aren't you always the one that sings 'God Special-izes?'" Martha asked pointedly, her gaze unwavering and knowing.

Layla lowered her eyes and focused on the table. She'd spent many Sundays singing in the church choir, imploring people with her notes to trust God. And she did really believe that He could do the impossible. But this… She couldn't risk another heartbreak.

"Yes, but God also said don't be foolish. It would be irresponsible for me to forget everything Linc did to this family. And I won't do that to my kids."

Layla stood abruptly, nearly tipping the chair over. She stalked over to the sink and filled up her stock pan with water. Once she set the pan on the stove, she turned it on and went to work peeling potatoes for the homemade French fries.

Behind her, she heard Martha shuffle into the family room, and make a squealing noise to Courtney. More shuffling and she figured Martha had finally laid little Linc down. Layla thought about the rainy night she went into *real* labor with her son, how scared she'd been when her water broke while she was alone yet again. Linc had been out of the house for two weeks at that point, had checked himself into a rehabilitation center somewhere upstate. But it wasn't until her water broke that reality had set in.

A frantic daddy-to-be hadn't wheeled her into the hospital at the last minute. Linc didn't stand near her head in the birthing room, holding her hand and assuring her that everything would be okay like he'd done with Courtney years before.

Her cold reality then was the same one she'd faced every day since. Instead of raising her children in a loving home with two parents, she was alone with two toddlers. There were days when she wasn't sure sanity was within her grasp, but she'd kept moving, kept working, kept loving on her kids.

She'd made the hard decision, walking away and changing the locks on their home. In the months that followed the intervention as she called it, she didn't ask any questions about him. Some would say she was cold-hearted, but she called it a protective instinct. It was hard enough getting up in the mornings, going through life putting on a brave face for her children and her students, for her sisters and brothers. She had to let go just to be able to live through the heartache.

Ma had tried to give her updates on Linc's progress every time they'd spoken to one another, but she would always change the subject. The letters he'd written to her remained unopened in her bedside table drawer. The only thing she had done was send pictures of the kids through Ma.

Layla sucked in a deep breath, and told herself she wasn't going to cry. She felt Ma come up behind her. She dropped the knife on the counter and dropped her head.

"It's okay to ask, Layla. It doesn't make you weak to care."

Closing her eyes, Layla allowed a sob to break free. Tears streamed down her face, and she turned to face Martha. Without another word, the older woman pulled her into a tight embrace. And Layla finally let go and cried —for her daughter who missed her daddy, for her son who'd never known his daddy, for the void that Linc had left in her heart, and for her failed marriage.

When the tears subsided, she pulled back and Martha brushed her thumbs under Layla's eyes. "I love you like you're my own, Layla. I'm always going to be here for you."

Layla nodded. "I know, and I thank you for it. How is he?"

Smiling, Martha told her the latest about Linc. The doctors were optimistic that he would remain clean and Linc had emerged as one of the more positive influences at the rehabilitation center on the western side of Michigan, nearly two hundred miles away from her in Ypsilanti. Linc had been such a good patient, that he'd started to mentor newer patients, and had volunteered to become a sponsor once he was back home.

It made Layla feel hopeful that Linc could beat this. Still, it didn't change anything for them. Despite his progress, she had to keep the boundaries set. "That's good to hear," she responded once Martha finished with her update. "I'm glad he's doing well."

"He'll be home soon, and I know he wants to see you. In one of the letters he wrote to me, he quoted the song that always reminds him of you."

Layla didn't need Ma to tell her the song. She knew it was a song by the Chi-Lights called "Have You Seen Her?" Once, he'd confessed that he'd heard that song in his head every time he thought of her because the words rang true for him. The knowledge that he saw her face everywhere he went had made her swoon. It didn't take long for her to fall in love with him after that.

"I remember," Layla admitted. Emotion threatened to take her breath away, so she turned her back on Martha and started peeling potatoes again.

Martha joined her, picking up a potato and grabbing a knife from the drawer. No more words were spoken. They finished preparing the food for the party together in silence.

An hour later, the streamers had been hung from the ceiling, the food prepared, Courtney's energy was on level ten, and Lil Linc was crying. But it felt normal to Layla. Her sisters had arrived with her nieces and nephews and the party would start on time.

Layla finished icing the cake she'd made and set it on the countertop. She couldn't wait to watch her baby boy dip his little hand into the cake. She'd loaded her camera with film, and was excited to capture the moments.

Lil Linc, with his big cheeks and deep dimples, crawled over to her and lifted his hands. She bent low and scooped him into her arms. "Are you excited, baby boy? You get to eat cake and ice cream today." He laughed and tugged at her dark curls.

Courtney ran over to her and wrapped her arms around Layla's legs. "Mama, can I eat some cake?"

Layla ran a finger over Courtney's cheek. "Not right now. We'll have plenty of time for cake."

The sound of the doorbell pierced the air. Martha shouted that she would get it before disappearing around the corner. A few minutes later, Martha appeared in the doorway to the kitchen, a weird look on her face.

Frowning, Layla asked, "Are you okay, Ma? Who was at the door?"

"Hi, LaLa."

Layla gasped. Standing behind Martha was Linc.

Lincoln Wilson had learned many things about life, about himself, about love and sacrifice over the past year. But one of the hardest lessons to learn had nothing to do with his addiction. He had taken for granted that Layla would always be there, that she would keep loving him despite his mistakes.

He'd survived the pain of withdrawal, learned to cope with isolation from everyone he loved. But being served with divorce papers had nearly brought him to his knees. After countless hours of individual and group therapy, meditation and prayer, he'd emerged from the pits of despair with clarity and a renewed determination to make it home to his family.

It felt like it had taken forever to get there, but Linc knew it was worth the rough journey. Every struggle, every tear, every compulsion to give up was worth this moment. He now stood before Layla stronger than he'd been in years.

With wide eyes, Layla retreated back a step, her arms tightening around his squirming son. *My son*. Other than pictures sent to him by his mom, he hadn't seen his kids. He'd already missed too much, more than he ever thought he'd miss from his own children's lives.

"Hi, LaLa," he said again. He held out a wrapped gift box.

Her mouth dropped open, before she closed it. "Linc." Her voice was a whisper, but it still sounded like a sonnet. "You're here?"

Linc placed the box on the kitchen table when Layla made no movement to grab it from him. "I heard you were having a little party for Lil Linc."

"I told him about it, Layla," Ma added. "I hope that's okay."

Nodding, Layla cleared her throat. "It's fine. You could have warned me, though."

Ma squeezed his arm and he knew he'd hear about this later. Because despite what she'd said, Ma didn't tell him to come. In fact, she'd strongly suggested he stay away. Of course, he hadn't listened. But he could never regret seeing his family.

"I could have," Ma told Layla. "But with everything that we talked about earlier, I didn't."

Linc scanned the room, not surprised that everyone had gone silent at his entrance. Surprisingly though, there were no glares from the people in attendance, no looks of disgust directed his way. Judging by the smiles and the encouraging nods, he'd venture a guess that they were happy to see him.

The baby in Layla's arms wailed, struggling to get out of her hold. Finally, she set him down and he crawled right over to him. Smiling, he bent down and picked up his son, hugging Lil Linc to his chest.

"Hi, son." Linc rocked his boy in his arms, taking in the baby lotion on his skin and the soft smell of shampoo in his hair. "I'm your daddy." His eyes locked on Layla's for a minute before dropping his gaze to the beautiful girl, standing behind Layla's leg.

Layla dropped to her knees and turned his daughter to face her. "Courtney, there's your daddy. Do you remember him?"

Linc waited for Courtney to say something, anything. His baby girl glanced up at him, a question in her brown eyes. But she didn't address him. Instead, she buried her face in her mother's chest.

Layla kissed the top of Courtney's head. A pang of hurt pierced his heart. When he'd made the decision to crash the party, he'd gone over many possible scenarios. He knew he was taking a chance showing up without notice, but he'd been home for a day and he'd been coming apart at the seams. He couldn't wait another minute to see Layla, to see his children.

Finally, Courtney pulled away from Layla and turned to him. "Daddy?" He closed his eyes at the sound of her high-pitched voice.

"Yes, I'm your daddy, girly-girl."

Courtney took a few tentative steps toward him, and he bent low with Lil Linc still in his arms. "Daddy," she repeated. She pinched his cheek, like she'd done so many other times in the past.

He picked her up with his other arm and stood to his full height. The cute little toddler he left was now a four-year old with her own mind. Smiling at her, he asked if she remembered him.

"Yes!" she shouted before hugging his neck.

Closing his eyes, he allowed himself a minute to bask in the warmth of his children's love. A moment passed before they both wanted to be let down to run around. Once they disappeared, he focused on Layla, who'd been watching him curiously.

"Can we talk?" she asked.

He nodded his response.

She led him into the Rec Room, off the kitchen. When they'd moved into the house, he'd turned the attached one-car garage into a little room where the kids could play. It was a small part of the total remodel of the house they'd done a few years back. He glanced at the detached two-car garage behind the house that he'd built, and noticed the Burgundy Oldsmobile parked in there.

"You got another car?"

Layla nodded. "I couldn't afford the note on the Ford Taurus you got me, so I traded it in for a used car."

Linc hated to hear that. One of the things he'd promised her was that he'd always give her what she needed. He still remembered the day he'd brought home the brand new Ford Taurus. The gleam in her eyes and the special thank you she'd given him later that night was tattooed in his memory.

And as he took her in, from head to toe, he realized the light in her eyes was gone. "I'm so sorry, LaLa."

Layla sighed and took a seat on one of the chairs at a card table. "It's okay. I've had to learn to live on a budget, which is a good skill to have. We get by."

"Get by" wasn't a phrase that he ever wanted to hear her say again. Walking up to the house, he'd noticed several things had gone undone—the grass hadn't been freshly cut, the bushes overgrown, and one of the gutters hung loose. All things he would have taken care of, but he'd dropped the ball. He'd let her down.

"While I'm glad you're back, I'm not sure showing up today was the best idea." Layla crossed her arms in front of her chest. "There're too many people here to discuss what needs to be discussed. Plus, I don't want to take away from Lil Linc's birthday. He deserves a fun day."

"I agree with you," he told her. "I want him to have a good day. I won't stay, but I had to see you. I had to see my babies."

Layla averted her gaze, picking at the hem of her shirt. "You don't have to go," she grumbled. "They're your children, too. I would never keep you away from them. But I wanted to let you know that we need to have a conversation about the kids. Just not today."

Linc couldn't help the smile that tugged at his lips. The fact that she didn't kick him out was a positive step. "I'll take it. I've missed so much already."

With a heavy sigh, Layla stood. "We should cut the cake."

Before he could respond, she turned and walked out of the room.

TWO

Layla rushed to the door, nearly tripping on a Barbie doll lying on the floor. Grumbling a curse, she picked it up and tossed it on the nearby couch. The kids were screaming in the Rec Room, playing with her teenage niece, Shante. And she was going to be late for her…date.

Swinging the door open, Layla prepared herself to offer apologies to Marvin for not being ready on time. However, the excuses died on her lips. It wasn't Marv at the door, but Linc. "Hi," she breathed.

She hadn't seen him in two weeks, since the day of Lil Linc's party. But they'd chatted on the phone several times about visits to the kids. With the school year winding down, she'd been busy marking papers and getting ready for exams. For extra money, she'd agreed to coach the soft-ball team, which often brought her home too late for him to come for a visit.

"Hey." He reached out and ran a finger over one of her curls, a gesture that used to make her tremble with anticipation. *It still did.* "You look beautiful."

"Thanks," Layla said, her voice shaky. "I decided to use the roller set last night."

"I tried to call, but I couldn't get through."

Layla shook her head. "Your son yanked the phone off the receiver. I had no idea it was off the hook until I went to call Sissy."

Sissy was her oldest sister and best friend. She was also the heart of the family. To know her was to love her.

"I hope you don't mind me stopping by. I wanted to spend some time with the kids. I want them to know me."

"No, I don't mind. I think it's good that you want to bond with them."

They stood there for a moment, staring at each other.

"Are you busy?" he asked.

"Oh, I'm sorry. Come in." She held the door open and let him in. He brushed past her and she fought the urge to lean in and sniff him. He always smelled divine. Today was no exception as she caught the hints of cedar wood, jasmine, and musk.

He looked good, too. Dressed in freshly pressed blue jeans and a dress shirt, he looked as fine as he ever did. And healthy, too.

"The kids are in the Rec Room with Shante," she told him. Shante was Linc's late sister's daughter. Ma had raised Shante most of her life, and Layla had developed a close relationship with her.

His gaze traveled up the length of her body, and the intensity of it seemed to awaken parts of her that had been asleep for over a year. She shifted on her feet.

"Going somewhere?"

This conversation wasn't going to be easy. Telling Linc she was going on a date somehow didn't feel right, even though she was free to see anyone she chose. "Um." She cleared her throat and pulled at her ear. "I'm going on a date."

He drew in a sharp breath, before schooling his features. It was a Linc move that she'd appreciated in the past. He'd always been composed, rarely lost his temper. Since he'd left, though, she'd often wished that he'd been a little more upfront with his feelings. Maybe it would have helped him cope with life instead of turning to drugs.

"A date," he repeated after a moment. "I didn't know you were seeing anyone."

She bit her lip. "It's not a big deal. One of my colleagues asked me out a few times."

"Do I know him?"

Layla hesitated. Despite the fact that they were divorced, she didn't want to hurt Linc. Truth was, he did know her date. They'd all gone to the same college together. In fact, Linc and Marv were members of the same fraternity. "Yes," she admitted on a sigh. "It's Marvin. You remember him from college."

"Ah." He opened and closed his fists several times before adding, "I remember him. I always knew he had a crush on you."

"I doubt that. We both did a lot of work in the Michigan Education Association this past school year. One day he asked me out, and I accepted."

During her years of teaching middle school, Layla worked tirelessly in the Teacher's Union. Recently, she'd been elected president of her local chapter. As a result, she'd traveled to Lansing, Michigan numerous times for meetings at the state headquarters.

"Glad to hear you're still working on the Union. They need people like you who are willing to fight for what's right."

Recent changes in the economy and the hard stance on

organized labor by President Reagan made her job unbearable at times. Couple that with the negative perception of high-ranking union members and the growing number of younger workers who felt unions were no longer necessary; it felt like an uphill battle.

"I try. I'm thinking of stepping down next year."

"You love the work. And it's important."

A smile tugged at the corners of Layla's mouth. Linc had always been supportive of her career and had even encouraged her to think bigger than merely teaching at a school. He'd challenged her to think of opening her own school.

Layla was one of the few people she knew that actually enjoyed going to work. Being able to mold young minds and prepare her students for greatness meant the world to her. Linc had always understood that about her.

"How are things going since you've been back?" Layla asked, changing the subject. "I know we haven't been able to schedule a visit with the kids, but I hope you've been keeping yourself busy."

"I started work again Monday."

Her hand flew to her chest. "Really? Where?"

"They hired me back at the plant."

Prior to Linc's troubles, he'd worked as a Skilled Trades laborer for one of the big automotive companies in the area. Jobs at the "plant" had afforded many African American people a good life.

"That's great, Linc."

"I don't work at the same building. I asked to be transferred to Rawsonville Road."

There were two huge manufacturing plants in their hometown of Ypsilanti. The previous location was only five miles for their home. The Rawsonville Plant was a little farther, but still not too big of a distance from home. Well, her home that is.

"May I ask why?" She leaned against the arm of the couch, careful not to wrinkle her dress.

"I didn't want to be in the same area, around the same people. One of my goals is to stay away from situations that aren't healthy for my recovery."

Her pulse raced at his admission. While he was away, she'd read up on the twelve steps of recovery. So she knew distancing himself from people or places that may tempt him to take a drink or more was important.

"And I got a place, too," he continued. "I couldn't stay at Ma's anymore. Too many people always there. It's not fancy, just two bedrooms and a bathroom. But it's closer to Ann Arbor, off of Washtenaw. Glencoe Hills."

Ann Arbor bordered Ypsilanti, and was home to the University of Michigan. Layla often drove to the neighboring town to shop at Arborland Mall or Briarwood Mall.

"I wanted to move away from my old stomping grounds." Linc shoved his hands into his pockets. "And I want my kids to feel safe when you finally decide to let them spend the night."

Layla knew the area well. It was quiet and peaceful over there, and she had no doubt it would be good for him. Although, Ma had a lovely, quaint home, it wasn't in the best area of Ypsi so she knew it would be hard for Linc to stay there.

"Good. Wow, I'm happy for you. It's a nice area."

He chuckled. "Remember we used to live near there?"

"I do." When they'd first married, they moved into a one-bedroom apartment close to where he was now. She recalled long walks around the grounds and hot nights on their balcony.

"You wanted to make sure we lived on the top floor because you didn't want mice to get in."

Layla giggled. "Of course. I hate those little rodents."

"I know. How is your family?"

"Alright. Well, you saw Sissy and Gwen at the party."

"Right."

"Everyone else is doing well."

Growing up in a household of six children and only three bedrooms, Layla had no choice but to be close with her siblings. She'd shared a bed with her youngest sister until she moved out for college. Her parents weren't poor, but they also weren't rich. They had done a good job of keeping them clueless. Layla had no idea her parents even struggled until she was a grown woman with a family of her own. All she knew was the love they had for each other.

"Have you seen any of your cousins?"

Layla held her breath as he seemed to mull over her question. It was no secret that she didn't care for a large segment of Linc's family. It was also no secret that they couldn't stand her. One of his older relatives had once called Layla a "stuck-up bitch" to her face. Needless to say, she'd made it a point to stay far away from them after that.

However, Linc had been very close with his relatives. There were several cousins that he grew up with in Southwest Detroit. They'd practically cut their teeth together. Unfortunately, though, those same cousins were functioning drug abusers. On the outside, they held jobs and owned homes. But after hours, they partied hard, drinking alcohol and using other substances such as heroin and the deadly crack cocaine.

"They've called for me at Ma's house," he replied. "But I haven't taken any of their calls. They also invited me out to a party over the weekend. I turned the invitation down."

"Really?"

"You sound surprised."

"Honestly? I am." She sucked in a deep breath. "You forget I know you. I know how you get down."

Linc was the life of any party, and often wanted to hang out with his family. It had been a source of contention for them, sparking many arguments, some pretty bad. Layla would beg Linc not to go to the latest party and Linc would push back and accuse her of not wanting him to spend time with his cousin.

Eventually, he'd started going out every weekend, sometimes twice. Soon, he was coming home later and later, and many times not at all. Things came to a head when she'd caught him rifling through her purse. When she confronted him, he'd admitted he had a problem.

The one thing that Linc also did was tell her that he wanted help, that he didn't want to need his drug of choice so much. The use of crack cocaine spiked in the 1980s, destroying families in its wake. He'd once described the first high as a euphoria he'd never had again but kept chasing.

Layla loved Linc, so she'd done everything in her power to help him. They'd tried prayer, outpatient therapy and rehabilitation centers. They'd even tried hypnosis. Things steadily got worse, until the night she'd had to break into the drug house to pull a high Linc out.

When she'd stood outside the crack house that spring night, it had felt like she'd been stuck in a horrible nightmare. She still remembered the smell of the smoke, the trash littering the inside of the house, the dazed look in the men and women inside the house. Drugs were always something that someone else did, not her husband. She'd counseled students who dealt with parents on drugs, but never thought she'd be living with an addict.

The pain of those memories floated just beneath the surface. Layla didn't want to keep replaying the hurt over and over. She wanted to forgive. But it was easier said than done, and she wasn't sure she'd ever trust him again.

"Layla?"

She blinked. "Huh?"

He tilted his head to meet her gaze. "Are you okay? You zoned out."

"I'm fine," she lied. "Just thinking."

Linc pointed toward the Rec Room. "You said the kids were with Shante. It's pretty quiet in there."

Layla forced a laugh. "Trust me, it won't last. But you can go in there."

"Thanks, LaLa."

"Linc?" she called, stopping him in his tracks. "I don't mind if you spend time with the kids while I'm gone. You've missed a lot of time with them."

He gave her a Linc special, a smile so bright, so sexy, she felt dizzy. "I appreciate that, LaLa. I'll let you finish getting ready. Enjoy your date."

Linc twisted the knob on the spinner and watched as the arrow stopped on the number two. *Shit.* It was the second time he'd spun a low number. At this rate, the game would never be over.

"Two!" Courtney shouted with a wide, toothy grin. "You're going to lose, Daddy."

He mussed her hair. "You're probably right." But he moved his pawn up the ladder, making sure he counted out loud. Fortunately for him, he landed on a picture square and was able to climb up the ladder, which put him ahead of his pouting daughter.

"No," Courtney screamed. She crossed her arms and frowned. "No fair. You're beating me now."

Linc chuckled. When he first went away, Courtney barely talked. The most she would say at any time was "no." Now, his baby girl was speaking coherently, in full sentences. According to Ma, Courtney was the top student in her pre-school class. She knew how to draw and could count to 100 with no trouble. He was one proud father.

"Girly-girl, it's your turn. You might pass me up on this try."

Courtney took her turn and landed on the number five. They both counted her turn and she squealed as she climbed ahead of him. Off to the side, Lil Linc slept on a blanket and his niece Shante had disappeared to call her friend.

Linc sent up a silent prayer of thanks that he'd been able to spend time with the kids like this. He looked forward to more games, more experiences. He'd already decided to teach Courtney how to swim. She was at the age when it would be easy to teach her.

"Want to go swimming with Daddy soon?" he asked, as he took his turn.

"Yay!" Courtney yelled. "I like water, Daddy. Mommy told me she couldn't get her hair wet right now and I had to wait."

Linc barked out a laugh. "Your mommy is funny, huh?"

"Do you love Mommy?"

The question caught him off guard and he froze, hand on his game pawn. He met his daughter's curious gaze. "Of course, I love your mommy."

"Where were you?"

Linc was glad he was sitting down because his daughter

had essentially knocked the wind out of him. He swallowed. "I had to go away, Girly-girl. Daddy was sick."

"Sick? Did you have a fever?"

He smiled. "No."

"Did your throat hurt? Because Mommy said that you don't have to go to school when your throat hurts."

Chuckling, he shook his head. "It's a long story. Too long to tell you right now. But...come here." He held out his arms and she climbed onto his lap. "Listen very carefully, okay."

She nodded, pulling at the hair of his growing beard. "You have hair on your face."

"I know, baby. It's called a beard."

"Bird?" she repeated.

"No, bee-ard."

Courtney made a silly face. "I don't like that word."

Linc kissed her brow. "Well, I'll remember that in the future. Maybe I'll cut it off so you don't have to say the word anymore."

She gasped. "You can't cut it. You might cut your cheeks. That will hurt because cuts hurt."

"Oh, Courtney." He hugged her. "I love you so much."

"Like you love Mommy?"

"Not quite like that. But one thing I want you to know is I will never leave you again. And I'm sorry for going away for so lo..." He sucked in a shaky breath. "Long."

She looked into his eyes, almost like she could see something inside him. "Don't be sad, Daddy. I love you—" She held her arms out at her sides, "—this big." Then, she hugged his neck tightly.

A knock on the door interrupted their bonding moment and he glanced down at the still sleeping Lil Linc before he stood up with Courtney in his arms. He opened the door to find Sissy on the other side, holding a cake pan in her arms.

Her eyes lit up. "Hi, Linc." She walked right in. "I didn't know you'd be here. I just stopped by to drop Layla's cake pan off. She's planning to make me her famous Texas Sheet Cake tomorrow and I had her pan from the last time she made it."

Linc groaned. The thought of the double chocolate cake with pecans made his mouth water. Layla was an excellent cook, and he'd missed sampling her treats. *In more ways than one*. "I need a piece of that cake."

"Done." Sissy looked at Courtney, who had quietly watched their exchange. "Hey, niecy poo."

"Auntie Sissy, do you have a quarter?" Courtney asked.

Sissy pulled a quarter from her pocket. "I sure do." She dropped the coin into Courtney's waiting hand. "Now, go put it in your bank."

Linc set Courtney down and she raced out of the room. "So, she likes money, huh?" he asked Sissy.

"Of course. What woman doesn't?"

He laughed and hugged Sissy. "I've missed you and your sense of humor."

She nudged him with her hip. "Oh, hush." She was dressed in her work uniform. Although she was a teacher by trade like Layla, she drove the city bus during summer break. "You know I tell it like it is."

"Still driving for the city, I see." He grabbed the pan from her and walked into the kitchen. Linc hadn't lived there for a while, but he still knew where everything went. He set the pan in the cabinet. "How's life treating you?"

"Life is good, brother-in-law."

"Not according to the courts," he muttered.

Sissy leaned her hip against the counter. "Don't be here if you're not going to do the right thing, Linc."

He met her waiting gaze. The Johnson sisters were alike in many ways, from their golden skin to their big eyes. But they had very different personalities. Gwen was the fun one, always ready to go. Elizabeth, the serious one, tended to be a work-a-holic. She barely came around because she would always be at work, making money. Sissy had been the first family member Layla had introduced him to when they started dating and more down-to-earth. And she'd never made him feel anything less than welcome in their lives. They'd bonded over the years and he called her a friend.

Nodding, he said, "I know."

"Do you?"

"Yes. Losing her did something to me. It changed how I see things, motivated me to get my act together. I'm not the same man I was before all of this happened. I'm better."

"Good. But you should know it won't be easy."

"I know that, too. Layla has always been stubborn."

"She's more than that. She's hurt, heartbroken. I don't want to see her like that again, Linc. If you hurt her, I might have to cut you."

The tiny smirk on Sissy's face told him she was joking. But not really. "I understand. I don't plan to hurt her. I know I fucked up. But I'm ready to make amends."

"Have you told her this?"

He shook his head. "We haven't had that conversation yet."

Sissy crossed her arms over her chest. "Don't you think that should be your priority? You've been home for two weeks now."

"I planned to talk to her tonight, but she went on a date."

Laughing, Sissy, clasped him on his shoulder. "Oh,

yeah. The date. Well, something tells me that date is going to be over before nine o'clock."

"You think so?"

"Oh, I know so. Especially now that you're home."

Linc felt a surge of hope at Sissy's words. "You think I stand a chance?"

"I'd say you have more than a chance. It's a given, *if* you stay on the right path. Not that it won't be a long, hard road to forgiveness," she added. "You do have a lot to make up for. In the end, though, I do believe that there will be no denying your love for each other. It was plain to see at Lil Linc's birthday party."

"Thanks for that. I hope you can forgive me for hurting her, and you. I know you were disappointed in me. And I'm sorry."

Sissy grinned. "You don't have to apologize to me, but I appreciate it. I do forgive you, and I can see that you're sincere. That's what I've been waiting to see." She pulled a cup out of the dish rack, turned on the faucet and filled it up. After she gulped down the contents, she set the glass on the countertop. "I better get home. I have another long day tomorrow."

They embraced each other again. "I'll see you soon," he said. "Maybe we can get a game of Tonk going."

"I don't mind taking your money."

He barked out a laugh. Tonk was a card game they used to play. It wasn't big money, but they played for dimes. "In your dreams."

He heard keys in the front door lock and glanced over at Sissy.

"See," Sissy said, a mischievous smirk on her face. "What did I tell you? Date over."

THREE

Layla heard voices in the kitchen when she entered her home. Heading to the kitchen, she saw Linc and Sissy standing there, both with arms across their chests.

"Hey," she said, setting her purse on the kitchen table. "What's going on?"

Linc glanced at his watch. "I didn't expect you back this early."

Layla didn't expect to be back, either. Usually a date with Marvin meant good conversation and good food. Yet, Layla had been distracted with thoughts of Linc, of memories of better conversation and better food. She shrugged. "Dinner was good, but I'm exhausted. So, I asked him to bring me home."

And Layla didn't just end the date. Since Marvin had been a good friend to her, she had been honest about her emotional state since Linc walked in her door a few weeks ago. She'd told him that she appreciated his friendship, but couldn't see him again romantically.

Sissy let out a theatric yawn. "Well, woo. I'm so tired. I'm going to head on home to get ready for work tomorrow." She gave Layla a hug and a kiss on her cheek. "I'll call you tomorrow, Layla."

A few minutes later, Layla and Linc were alone. Well, as alone as they could be with two kids and Shante. At that moment, Courtney burst into the kitchen and wrapped her arms around Layla's legs.

"Mommy!"

Layla lifted her daughter into her arms and hugged her. "Hey, babe." She kissed Courtney's brow. "Did you have fun with Daddy?"

Courtney grinned at Linc. "Daddy played Chutes and Ladders with me. I was winning before Auntie Sissy came."

"You were kicking my butt, Girly-girl." Linc tickled Courtney's neck and her daughter giggled uncontrollably, squirming in her arms.

As Linc played tickle monster with Courtney, Layla couldn't help but let her eyes roam over her ex-husband. His brown skin looked healthy, his beard was neatly trimmed, and he had weight on his bones—a healthy weight.

A smile tugged at her lips. The man in front of her, playing with their baby girl, was the man she'd fallen hope-lessly in love with in college. This was the man that made her laugh, protected her above all others.

"So I take it you had a good night with the kids," she said. "Where's my boy?"

Linc pointed at the Rec Room. "He passed out a little while ago. Didn't want to move him. I just enjoy having them closer to me."

Layla nodded, before turning to Courtney. "Court, it's time for bed."

"No, Mommy." Courtney pouted. "I want to see Daddy."

"You can see Daddy tomorrow."

"Can Daddy tuck me in?"

Layla sighed. Turning to Linc, she ticked her head toward Courtney. "Do you mind? I'll grab Lil Linc and get him down."

"Sure," he said, grabbing Courtney and hoisting her up in his arms. Then, he took off at a run up the stairs, making an airplane noise as he "flew" her upstairs.

Several minutes later, Layla and Linc made their way downstairs back to the kitchen. "Coffee?"

"That would be nice," he said.

Shante had decided to stay the night, and in typical teenage fashion, had retreated to the basement to watch television. Layla put the teakettle on and pulled two mugs from the cabinet. She worked in silence, fully aware that Linc was watching her. It should have made her nervous, but instead it made her feel safe.

Once she finished with the coffee, she brought the mugs over to the table and joined him. "I figured you still took your coffee black."

"And you still take yours white."

Layla laughed. He used to tease her that she might as well have a cup of warm milk since she put so much cream and sugar in her coffee. "Stop."

"You went on a date," he said after a few moments.

Her eyes met his. "I did," she mumbled.

"I didn't like it. I hated it."

"Linc, we're divorced. Would you have me be alone for the rest of my life?"

"I would have you be with me for the rest of your life. And mine, too. Because my life without you is empty."

Unable to formulate a response to his declaration, she dropped her gaze and played with the hem of her shirt. He reached out and tipped her chin up to face him.

"I know now more than ever that if you don't learn from your mistakes, you're more apt to repeat them," he continued.

Layla traced the rim of her mug. "I don't know if I—"

"No, let me finish." He stood, and approached her. "I've learned that tomorrow isn't promised, so it's best to take the necessary steps today. I've been wanting to talk to you. There are some things I feel I need to say."

She knew the conversation was coming, but she didn't want to ruin the moment. The distance between them felt far and wide a few weeks ago. But every minute, every second he was there, seemed to chip away at her resolve and wake up her heart. His mere presence jolted her senses in a way that was unique to him, to them.

Layla had longed for him to be by her side. Now that he was there, she fought an internal battle with herself. Every part of her wished for a time machine, for a do over. Yet, the reality of the situation stayed in the back of her mind. She was afraid, terrified that the minute she counted on him, he'd do something to burn her again.

"LaLa." He grabbed her hand. "I just want to be honest with you. I've made so many mistakes. And part of my recovery is making amends."

"Linc, we don't have to do this."

"I do. LaLa, I'm so sorry. I'm sorry for the ways I've hurt you. I'm sorry for taking your trust in me, something so strong and lasting, and turning it to dust and letting it fly away with the wind. I want to earn it back. Please, let me try."

Layla's eyes burned and her throat closed up. Because, *what can I say to that?*

"And the only way we can get past this is for us to be honest with each other. So, I need you to be honest with me."

Layla wasn't sure what he was asking, but she didn't see this conversation going well if she told him everything. "How is that going to help?"

"It helps. I know I fucked up, LaLa. But you didn't tell me how I hurt you. You just left."

"You promised me you would love me, keep me, and protect me. In front of God and our families, you vowed to be there! I left because you broke those promises. You betrayed my trust!" Layla shouted. She slapped a hand over her mouth and glanced at the stairs. "I'm sorry."

"Don't be sorry. I don't want you to be sorry. The only sorry person here should be me."

Layla stood, needing distance between them. "Every time we fought, every promise broken, destroyed a piece of me that I'm not sure can be fixed." She leaned against the countertop, needing the support. "I love you. There's no doubt about that."

"I love you, too."

"But the question is can I forget about the hurt and pain? Can I put that all aside and take the risk to be with you again? You said I left you, but you left me first."

"LaLa, I never would have left you. I didn't leave you."

"But you did. Not physically, but emotionally. You let that substance become Lord of your life. You stole from me. You ruined us." Her chin trembled. "I would have done anything for you. But you did too much, took too much. I gave you so much of myself and you squandered it."

"I know. I'm so sorry, baby, and I want to make it up to you. I want to be the man you fell in love with."

She held her hand up when he approached her. "Don't come closer. I told you we shouldn't do this." The anger, the hurt, every emotion she'd felt over the last few years churned in her gut and she wanted to lash out at him for making her feel this way. "Linc, you can't make it up to me. The only thing I need from you is for you to take care of your kids, for you to be a father to them. As far as us… we're done. I can't go back."

"And I can't go back to living without you. I need you."

"Linc, you were my love. It doesn't matter how much time has passed, or who comes in or out of our lives. It doesn't even matter that I haven't seen you in a year. You'll always be that for me. But you're asking me to forget everything that's happened to give you a chance. You want me to open myself up for that soul crushing hurt again."

"I'm asking you to give me a chance, to come back to me. I promise to give you everything you need. I won't let you down, baby."

"Linc, it's too much, too soon. I told you I wasn't ready to have this conversation. Gosh, I told you."

It didn't matter how much he'd hurt her, how many nights she'd spent crying over him and for him, she hated to see the devastation in his eyes. She wanted to comfort him, she wanted to believe him.

"You don't trust me," he said. "And I get it. But my life, all of my recent accomplishments mean nothing without you. I've worked very hard to get here. I've beat the odds and I'm not going back." He tugged her to him, and she gasped. "Layla, please." He leaned his forehead against hers. Tears fell from his eyes.

"Linc, don't," she whispered.

Nuzzling her nose, he leaned forward. "I'm so sorry I hurt you, that I broke us. I just need you to forgive me. Please… I love you so much," he whispered against her lips.

Desire spread through her, even as she wanted to push him on his ass. He was so close and he smelled so good. With his eyes on hers, he closed the tiny gap and took her mouth in a soft kiss. It wasn't desperate or frantic, it was tender and sweet and loving. It was everything. She wanted to give in, she wanted to drape herself in him. But…

She pulled away and wiped her mouth. "Don't do that again."

"Why not?"

"Because…" she shook her head, ran a frustrated hand over her face. "I can't do this. Not again. But what I can do is let you spend more time with the kids."

Layla walked away and plopped into her chair. She took a moment to steady herself and took a quick sip of her cold coffee.

A few seconds later, he joined her. "Okay. We can talk about a schedule."

She peered at him then, unsure what she expected to see. Maybe more hurt? Maybe despair? Maybe something indicating that he would go out and seek a high because of her rejection? She didn't see any of those things, though. Linc appeared strong and sure.

He smiled. "I definitely want to spend time with my children. They're part of the reason I'm here. Nothing will ever change that."

"Good. Because they need you." *I need you.*

"I'll be here. I won't let them down…or you."

They spent the next several minutes planning out visits, and Layla was grateful for the change in subject. Talk of their relationship had drained her as much as it had reinforced what she'd known all along. Linc would be the only man for her. Nothing really mattered but him and the family they'd created.

She felt lost without him, and she wanted to believe in him, have faith in their love. But she knew that if he hurt her again, she would be no good to anyone else. And she couldn't go down that road because she had children who depended on her to be there.

Linc finally stood and set his mug in the kitchen sink. "I'd better go. I'm moving tomorrow. I want you to come and see my place, so you can be assured that it's in good shape."

Layla followed Linc to the door and tried not to look at his butt. Lost in her thoughts, she had no idea he'd stopped walking until she rammed into him. She nearly toppled over, but his strong arms wrapped around her, holding her up.

She peered up at him. "I'm sorry. I was thinking about something."

He chuckled. "I do that a lot around you, too."

A blush worked its way up her neck. "Linc." She rolled her eyes. "You're too conceited for your own good."

Linc had a magnetic personality. It was one of the first things she'd noticed about him all those years ago. They'd met when she'd purchased him at her sorority's slave auction. The fundraiser had been held every year on campus. And when Linc stepped out on the stage with his suit on, Layla didn't hesitate to bid all the money in her purse—twenty-five dollars—to win a date with him.

Little did she know, that money would be the best money she'd ever spend. Because despite the state of their relationship now, she couldn't regret the good times they'd had, the babies they'd created from their love.

"You love it." He winked at her. "So, I'll call you when I'm all settled and you can bring the kids by."

"Sounds like a plan," she said.

He turned to open the door and she reached out to stop him before she could talk herself out of it. "Linc, wait." He had been honest with her, so she wanted to return the favor.

His gaze dropped down to her hand on his arm. "Yes."

"About my date? I told Marv I couldn't see him again. He's a nice man, but it wasn't right to keep stringing him along."

"Good. I would hate for you to keep stringing him along, too."

Layla's mouth fell open. "What?"

"I'm glad you realized that I'm the only man for you."

She giggled nervously. "Linc, this doesn't mean what you think it means. We're still over."

"I know." He smirked. "But I can't help but feel like this is a good sign."

"Linc, don't—this isn't us getting back together. We already had that difficult conversation."

"Right," he said, sarcasm evident in his tone. Picking up her hand, he brushed his lips over her palm. "I'll call you after I finish moving. I don't have a lot of things, so I can still come by and visit with the kids. That way, you can have time to write your lesson plans for Monday."

Layla couldn't believe the turn this had taken. "But—"

He leaned in and kissed her cheek. "Bye, baby."

She sucked in a deep breath. "Linc, you—"

Placing a finger against her mouth, he said, "I'll see you tomorrow, LaLa."

Swallowing, she simply nodded and watched him strut out the door.

Linc walked through his apartment a week later, making sure he had everything in place. Layla would be there any minute with the kids for their first visit. He hadn't expected her to let them come so soon, but she'd called that morning and asked if he wouldn't mind a visit while she went to the hair salon. Of course, he'd agreed without hesitation. It was one more step closer to his end goal of building her trust in him again.

While Linc was away, he'd wondered if he could handle hate in Layla's eyes when she looked at him. But he didn't see hate when he peered into her brown eyes. Her orbs were clouded with hurt, sadness. But he'd also seen desire and hope.

He'd changed so much, learned so much about himself. Some things were good, others were bad. She'd told him the truth, about how he'd hurt her. The old Linc would have crumbled under the weight of her words and looked for his next high to dull the pain. The man he had become could take it. Because when all was said and done, he deserved it. He'd hurt her in unimaginable ways, and he was ready to atone for that.

Over the past week, he'd noticed progress in their relationship. They'd seen each other nearly every day since that hard conversation in her kitchen. As much as he'd hated seeing the hurt on her face, hearing it in her voice, he knew that talk had to happen. He'd learned that it was better to confront hard issues upfront and declare his intentions early on so there would be no confusion.

Each day, she'd smiled at him a little more, which he took as a good sign. They'd even shared iced tea and shortbread cookies on the back porch last night. It was like old times, sitting outside telling each other about their respective days.

Smiling, he remembered Layla's reaction to the news that he'd re-enrolled at Eastern Michigan University to finish his degree. Shock, awe, pride, and—*dare I say it*—love.

Although Layla and Linc met in college, he'd yet to graduate. Instead, he'd chosen the fast money of a full-time, well-paying job at the plant. After they married, they'd talked about him going back to finish his program, but Courtney came. Linc just didn't feel comfortable cutting back on his shifts and losing out on the overtime pay.

Linc had other aspirations, though. The plant was nice work, but he wanted more for his life. He'd gained valuable experience working on homes, and had a reputation in the community of being professional and expedient, while doing excellent work. Finishing his degree was step one in his goal of starting his own business.

Being so far away, disconnected from his family and so-called friends, he'd had a lot of time to think. Life was short and he didn't want to make the mistake of thinking he had time to do the things he wanted to do, or time to spend with Layla, Courtney and Lil Linc. He wanted to grab life and the many opportunities presented to him by the horns and make the best of it.

The loud sound of the buzzer brought him out of his thoughts. Excitement bubbled in his gut as he hurried to the door, pushed the button to let her in, and opened his door. He heard Courtney talking a mile a minute as they walked up the short flight of stairs. When he saw them hit the landing, he met them there, taking Lil Linc from her arms.

"How's my boy?" He lifted his dimpled boy in the air, barely avoiding the gob of drool that spurted out of his son's mouth as he laughed. "And my girly-girl?"

Courtney grinned up at him. "Daddy, I brought another game to play." She held out a box of cards. "It's called Old Maid. You're going to lose again."

He laughed. "I'm sure you'll beat me. Just wait until I teach you how to play Monopoly."

"Manpuly?" Courtney asked, a questioning look in her eyes. "What's Manpuly?"

"You'll learn soon enough," he told his daughter. Linc took a minute to look at Layla, who'd been watching the exchange quietly. "And how is Mommy?"

She covered her mouth, seemingly to hide the smile he knew was there. "Mommy is fine."

"Come on in." He led them into his apartment and set Linc on the carpet. "I wasn't sure if the kids ate, but I have hot dogs and Pork N' Beans."

Layla scrunched her nose. "Yuck. You know I hate those things."

"Good thing I'm not making them for you, baby."

She shoved him playfully. "You get on my nerves, Linc." She scanned the living room. "You have a nice place here. It's quiet. I noticed the park on our way in. Maybe you could take the kids over there. Courtney loves to swing."

"Yeah, Daddy." Courtney jumped up and down, giddy with excitement. "I want to go to the park."

"I will definitely take you to the park, Girly-girl. As soon as Mommy leaves, alright?"

Courtney squealed in delight before she dropped to the floor and opened up her box of cards. While she was preoccupied and Lil Linc was sucking his fist, Linc turned to Layla. "They're alright here. Don't worry."

Her gaze softened. "I'm not worried, Linc. I know you'll take good care of them."

"Take your time. I don't have any plans today."

"That's actually good to know. I have to run several errands."

She kissed both kids, waved at him, and left.

A few hours later, both kids were down for a nap and

Linc had dinner on the stove. He'd planned to ask Layla to stay for dinner when she came.

Layla arrived just as he'd finished with dinner and he grinned when she stepped into the apartment and groaned. "Smells so good. What did you make?"

Ma had taught Linc to cook at his request. He was her only son that actually had a desire to learn and Ma had been happy to pass her recipes down to him. "Cubed steak with gravy, rice, and green beans."

"Yum."

"Can you stay for dinner?"

She took a step back. "I don't know, Linc."

"Just dinner," he assured her. "Besides, the kids are asleep. They played so hard at the park, they couldn't keep their eyes opened.

"Okay, I'll stay."

FOUR

"Have a seat." Linc pulled out Layla's chair and waited until she took a seat to go to the kitchen. He made quick work of setting their plates. Once he'd finished, he brought a full plate over to her and set it in front of her. He took the seat across from her and they started their meal.

Layla cut a piece of her steak and dipped it in the gravy before popping it in her mouth. She hummed as she chewed. "Linc, you definitely know your way around a kitchen. I can never beat your cubed steak and gravy."

He pointed his fork at her. "Just like I could never beat your pepper steak and your chicken and rice."

She giggled. "You're funny."

"Or your tuna casserole. By the way, can you make me one?"

"Really?"

"Yes," he admitted. "I dreamed of your cooking while I was away."

"Okay, I'll make one soon and have you over for dinner." She looked at her plate. "The kids would love that."

"Would my kid's mother love that?"

She dropped her fork onto her plate and scooted her chair back from the table. "Linc, we've been through this before."

"Okay, I'll stop. Just eat."

They finished dinner is silence, tension filling the air. Deciding to break the silence, he said. "Remember when we first started dating, how we spent so much time on the phone?"

She glanced up at him, a soft smile on her face. "I do. Sometimes, we even fell asleep on the phone. My room-mate used to get so angry with me."

"I'd never been a talker, but I couldn't let you get off the phone."

At the time, it had surprised him how much he'd loved taking to her. Her voice was like a balm to his soul. Ma did her best while they were growing up, but they'd grown up in a part of town rife with drugs and violence and death. Sure, it was a close-knit community where everyone knew each other, still it had a seedy side that made growing up hard.

Smoking cigarettes and marijuana, drinking alcohol, or using drugs were accepted activities of his peers. All of his friends had dabbled in drugs. Close family members of his had gotten strung out on drugs long before he even tried them. He'd even lost several people to overdoses.

Layla had shown him a different way to live. She'd given him a way out of that life with her love. But he'd messed up anyway. He really had no excuse. Yes, he was a product of his environment, but he had choices. He didn't have to end up like so many others. He didn't have to succumb to the pressure. It had taken a long time to stop dwelling on what he did and focus on what he wanted to do, how he wanted to make things right.

"I want to thank you for being the person you are, Layla," he told her.

He'd spent hours thinking back in time to happier days while in rehab, picking out pieces of their life together to hold on to. It was the only thing that had kept him sane during the hard withdrawals and loneliness.

"You've never made a promise you didn't keep. I remember you said you were going to quit smoking."

They had gathered at a distant cousin's home for a party and Layla announced to the entire room that she planned to quit smoking the next day. No one believed her, but he did. Because when she said she was going to do something, she did it. Her strength was one of the things he'd loved about her. True to her word, she'd thrown out her last pack of cigarettes before she finished them and never picked up another one again. Cold turkey. He'd often wished he had her willpower then.

"And you're the reason I'm still alive. You and our kids."

Her hand flew to her chest. "Linc, I appreciate what you're saying. But you have to give yourself some credit. You did the work to get clean. Now, you have to do the work of staying clean. No one can do that for you."

"You're right. That's definitely one of the things I learned there. I had to decide to stop everything that might lead me to relapse. I quit smoking cigarettes. I quit drinking. And I will stay sober."

"I'm glad you had something to hold on to, Linc. I prayed for you every day. I still do."

Linc let his gaze travel over her. Layla wasn't like other girls or women he'd been with and that drew him to her. Her beauty was irrefutable. Sometimes, he'd just stare at her and wonder why she'd chosen him, why she loved him.

He noted her freshly curled hair, the streak of blond in

her long tresses. Her expressive eyes and her full lips had filled his daydreams. It was little things about her that drove him crazy with need. Like the dimple on her left cheek, her melodic laugh, the way her hand felt in his, or even the smell of her skin.

They'd bonded over music, over education, over the need to build something lasting. They'd laughed for no reason and spent hours playing board games or ping pong. Traveling was a priority in their relationship as well. Summer had been their time to visit family down south or take trips to Toronto, Canada with friends. They had even visited the amusement park, Cedar Point, once a year.

"I was thinking, maybe we could drive the kids to Cedar Point this summer. Courtney would love the kiddie rides, don't you think?"

She nodded. "I think so. That would be nice."

Located on Lake Erie in Sandusky, Ohio, Cedar Point was one of the oldest amusement parks in the United States. And it was only a two-hour drive from Ypsilanti. Linc figured they could pack a lunch and drive there for the day.

"I heard the new water park, Soak City, is fun. We could make a day of it."

"Count me in," she said with a wide grin. "We haven't been there in so long."

"I'll plan everything. Just let me know what dates work best for you."

"I'm free after mid-June."

Linc figured the best time to go would be around Independence Day. In the past, they would spend the holiday with friends and family, but he wanted to be sure his circle was free of negative influences so he'd planned to forgo any holiday festivities that year.

"I'll call you once I finalize plans. Or just tell you when I visit the kids."

"Good." She sighed heavily, and stood. "I'd better get the kids ready. We have an early day tomorrow."

"Really? What do you have planned?"

"Going to visit Gwen and her kids. I've been promising to come out for a long time."

"Sounds like a good time." Panic rose in him as she headed toward the second bedroom where the children were sleeping.

"Layla?" he called.

She stopped and turned to him, a question in her eyes.

He approached her slowly. "Do you still love me?"

"You know I love you."

Linc knew he might be taking a chance that she would bolt before he was ready to let her go. But he kept going. "Are you still in love with me?"

"It doesn't matter."

"Yes, it does. I once told you that you were home. My place is with you. No one else. You told me that you felt the same."

"I did."

"I believe you still do. Once you find your home, no one else will fill that void. That's why you broke it off with Marvin. Because you know there is no other man for you."

"This is a moot point, Linc. Loving you is one thing. Trusting you is another."

"I don't want to waste any more time, LaLa. Tell me you can forgive me."

She held his face in her hands. "I do love you, Linc. I forgive you. Now, forgive yourself and move on. We can be great friends and loving parents to our children."

"Is that what you really want?"

Layla placed a sweet kiss to his lips and his heart

cracked wide open at her touch. He'd dreamed about it. The feel of her lips on his, the thought of her possible forgiveness had sustained him through the months in recovery.

When she pulled away, he wanted to tug her closer. He wanted to feel her tongue against his, take her into his bedroom and worship her body the way he knew she liked it.

She kissed his cheek. "It is what I want." Then, she pulled away and walked into the bedroom.

Her words had hollowed him out, but her actions gave him hope. The fact that she'd forgiven him and then kissed him filled him with a joy he hadn't felt in years. Although he couldn't change what happened, he could be the man she needed. If he didn't give this his all, he'd regret it. So, he decided in that moment to stay close, to convince her to take that chance on him. But he'd change his tactic a little bit. He sensed Layla needed to feel some control over this situation, so he'd let her come to him. And he felt confident she would.

Layla walked back in the living room, searching for something. Her gaze settled on the corner of the room where he'd stashed the children's bags. She ventured that way and picked them up. On her way back to the room, he halted her tracks with his hand on her arm.

"I miss you more than I can even say." It was his fault that they weren't together, that he couldn't touch her the way he wanted to or hold her in his arms, but he couldn't dwell on his mistakes anymore. Words without actions were meaningless. And Linc didn't want to spend the rest of his life missing her. So, he would do everything in his power to spend the rest of his life loving her.

"I know."

Pulling her to him, he smiled at the dazed look in her

eyes. He cupped her cheeks with his palms and kissed her brow. "I don't want to make you uncomfortable. I'm going to give you the space you need. I won't come to you again, asking for another chance for us." She opened her mouth to respond, but he forged ahead. "I'll continue to be the father that our kids deserve, but I won't force you to be with me."

She frowned. "Why? I mean, why the change?"

"Because I'm a believer." He traced the line of her bottom lip with his thumb, encouraged by the way her eyes fluttered closed. "I know we're not done, not by a long shot. But you're going to have to come to me. You're going to have to make the first move. Until then, I'll focus on rebuilding our friendship. You were my best friend, LaLa. You still are. I've already told you that I want to be with you and our kids. I want to love you. And I want you to let me. But it's your call, your pace."

Linc kissed her hard and fast before he let her go and walked into the bedroom to get the kids ready.

Layla had spent her last day in the classroom giving hugs and wiping the salty tears of her students as they progressed to the next level of their education. One of her "kids" screamed when his parents came to pick him up from school. Another had to be pried from her desk.

It was hard saying goodbye, but she'd assured them she would see them next year for sure. The seventh grade classes were just down the hall, so it wouldn't be forever. Still, she felt honored to be adored by the kids she'd taught all year.

Yet, despite her love of the job, she found herself looking forward to the summer every year. It was a time to rest, recuperate from the pressures of the classroom. The best part? Spending time with her family. Courtney would be starting Kindergarten in the fall, and Lil Linc changed in some way every single day.

On the way home, she stopped and grabbed a few Mr. Misty's from Dairy Queen, one for her and one for Courtney to celebrate. When she turned on her street, she noticed Linc's car parked in front of the house and a Sears truck out front. She pulled into the driveway and walked around the side of the house, back to the front where she'd seen Linc standing and chatting with a worker.

"What's going on, Linc?"

He pointed at the roof. "Those were the original gutters on the house, and they needed to be replaced. And since it was also the original roofing, I paid to have them replace that as well. They'll come and update the siding in a few weeks, after you choose the color you want."

Layla's mouth fell open. "What? You bought new gutters, a roof, and siding?"

He shrugged. "It was needed. I worked a lot of over-time last week and I had a Sears account."

She stared at him in disbelief. "What? You didn't have to do that."

"I know I didn't. And I know I signed over the house and everything in the divorce, but I want to be make sure you and the children are safe. So, I'm doing what I would have done if I still lived here."

"Where are the kids?"

"Ma came and got them. The noise was getting to Lil Linc. I hope that's okay."

Layla shrugged. "It's fine."

"Good." He smiled. "How was your last day of school?"

"It was good. I'm tired, though. I have to clean up my classroom next week."

"I can come help if you want."

Layla thought about telling him no, but decided against it. He'd kept his promise of not talking to her about their relationship and hopes of getting back together. Not since the dinner they'd shared at his house weeks ago.

"Sure. If you have time. I know you've been working hard."

"I'll make time."

The last several weeks had gone by quickly. They'd both had other obligations, that had kept them busy. Yet, even though he'd been working hard studying for his summer class and working overtime at his job, he'd made time to come see her and the children.

Every week, he'd come over to cut the grass. He'd also painted the Rec Room on one of his off days. On pay days, he would bring her over money to help support the children. The house had slowly been transformed due to his care and attention. And Layla appreciated his presence on a daily basis. The kids loved him being around as well.

Linc had bought Courtney and Lil Linc tool kits so they could "help" him around the house. Courtney had lost interest fairly quickly, preferring to play with her dolls. But Lil Linc enjoyed banging his plastic hammer in time with his daddy.

Layla handed Linc Courtney's drink. "I bought this for Courtney, but she's not here. Don't want it to melt."

He took it and grinned at her. "Thanks. Appreciate it. Why don't you go on in and relax? I'll handle this. They're basically just setting up today. The real work will begin tomorrow. I also contacted a heating and cooling specialist to come out and fix the central air conditioner."

"Linc, you're spoiling me."

He reached out and swiped the hair that had fallen in her face away. "Just doing my job. It's no trouble. I realize this house is a lot to maintain alone. I'm able to help, so I want to."

"Thanks," she said. "I'm going go on in and find something to eat."

She turned and walked into the house.

Later, Linc entered through the back of the house, calling her name.

"I'm in the Family Room," she shouted, her eyes on the television. She'd taken to playing Super Mario Bros. on the game system Linc had purchased last week for the kids.

He stepped down into the sunken room. "You like that, huh?"

"I do. I've been playing to wind down in the evenings, after I put the kids to bed. I still can't get past this water level, though. I keep getting bit by those little thingys."

Linc barked out a laugh, and Layla hit the pause button. "Are you laughing at me?"

"I am. You're addicted, and it's only been a week."

He sat next to her and she resisted the urge to lean into him. Layla had told him she wanted them to be friends and co-parent. At the time, she'd told herself it was necessary to let him down, to tell him that she didn't want to be with him anymore. It was a blatant lie. She wanted to believe in him. She wanted to be with him.

Linc grabbed the remote and started to play. In minutes, he beat the board and Layla forgot to be mad. Because he was so close, so male.

"Have you eaten?" he asked.

Layla blinked. "Huh?"

"I asked if you had eaten anything? Want to go get dinner?"

She eyed him. "You mean, together?"

Shrugging, he said, "Of course. But if you'd rather go separately, that's fine. I just want to be sure you've had something to eat."

"No, we can get something to eat." She stood and wiped her sweaty palms on her pants. "What do you have a taste for?"

"Chinese? The Mayflower restaurant on Michigan Ave?"

"Okay."

The restaurant was quiet, but they'd filled the silence with talk about the past, the present, and the future. Linc had told Layla about the summer class he'd been taking and she'd shared her challenges with the new principal at her school.

"I think you should tell her how you feel?" he suggested, cutting a piece of his Chicken Egg Foo Young. "It can only help you to be upfront with her."

"I don't know, Linc. I think it will make it worse. You know how I can get."

Layla knew her strengths and weaknesses. She also knew her priorities. They'd recently replaced her good friend and school principal with a control freak, one who coincidentally shared the same last name as she did. Layla and her friends called the woman "The Mean Ms. Johnson."

"I do know." He swiped a piece of sweet and sour chicken from her plate. "But it's better than suffering in silence."

"I'm not suffering," she argued. "It's not that serious to me. I have other things to consider."

"Maybe she's starting in on you because she knows you're the Union President."

Layla rolled her eyes. "That doesn't even make sense." Using her spoon, she took a spoonful of rice from his plate.

"If anything, she should know to leave me alone *because* I'm the head of the local."

"True. Well, you'll be able to better formulate a course of action while you're off this summer."

"Exactly. But my first plan is to sleep. Then, I want to take the children to Boblo Island."

Boblo Island Amusement Park was located on Bois Blanc Island in Ontario, Canada. It was only eighteen miles from Detroit and most Michiganders would take a huge ferry from Detroit to Boblo to enjoy the attractions.

"That's a good idea. I think Boblo may be a better option than Cedar Point because the kids are so young. Can I join you?"

"Yes, you can join us. But I still want to go to Cedar Point, but maybe we can add SeaWorld Ohio to the list. That can be a weekend trip."

He paused, fork midair. "Really?"

"Why do you sound so surprised? The kids would love SeaWorld. I can imagine Courtney's wide eyes and many questions."

"You're right about that. She is a pro at the questions."

"What time is Ma bringing the children back?" she asked.

Glancing at his watch, he told her Ma would bring the kids back around eight o'clock. "Which is soon, so we'd better get back to the house."

She placed her hand on top of his and squeezed. "Linc?"

His gaze locked on hers. "Layla."

"I had fun tonight. Thanks for bringing me here. I haven't had Mayflower since…" She didn't want to finish that sentence, because she didn't want to dwell on the past anymore.

"You can say it." He turned his palm up and entwined his fingers with hers. "I can take it."

"But I don't want you to take it, Linc. We've talked about this ad nauseum, and I don't want to keep talking about it. I want to continue to move forward."

"I'm glad you said that because I'm in total agreement."

"You've been wonderful these past several weeks, and I'm so grateful that you're strong and healthy. Even though we're not together, I've realized something that I'd tried to deny. What we meant to each other could never entirely disappear. Our lives are too entwined. We've been through so much together—fought so many battles, laughed so hard...loved even harder. That's nothing to be ashamed of."

"I agree."

Layla was sinking fast staring into his eyes. She saw the sincerity in them, felt the pull to him. Memories danced in her mind of the first time she'd seen him. Even then, one look from him seemed to unravel her.

"Okay, then. Let's get out of here." Standing, she grabbed her purse and smiled up at him. "Linc, you're a good man. Continue being who you are. I'm proud of you."

He leaned forward, resting his forehead on hers. "You don't know how much that means to me."

"I think I do," she whispered. "It means a lot to me, too."

He wrapped his arms around her, embracing her in the middle of the practically empty restaurant. He smelled like home. And for the first time since he'd come back, Layla let him hold her without pulling back.

FIVE

Linc pushed the heavy door open and stomped inside. Sighing, he scanned the area. The Elk's Frontier Lodge had been one of Linc's hangouts prior to his stint in rehab and he'd vowed to never return once he came home.

But when Ma called and asked him to find his youngest brother, Byron, he couldn't tell her no. Now, he was sure he'd made the wrong decision. He hadn't been to the bar in over a year, but as far as he could tell, nothing had changed. There wasn't much of a crowd at three in the afternoon, but a few of his old coworkers were sitting at the bar, nursing cold beers. More than likely, these men were still on the clock. Which wasn't all that surprising.

Working at the plant had made his life easier financially, but it had also made his life hard in other aspects. It was like a tiny city inside the walls of the manufacturer. Men had work wives, and vice versa. Drugs and alcohol were rampant and it wasn't hard to sneak away to go to the horse track or just to cheat on a spouse.

The toxicity of the environment was one of the reasons he'd requested a transfer to another plant. Yet, his current place of work was no different. Every morning, he told himself that it was only temporary, because walking into the sweltering hot hell he called a job had taken a toll on him.

Linc spotted Byron at the end of the bar, talking to a woman he recognized as trouble. Shaking his head, he headed over to his brother and told the woman to beat it before he slid on to the barstool next to him.

Byron glared at him. "I was wondering when I'd see you."

The last time Linc had seen his brother hadn't been pretty. The two had argued and even exchanged blows, all because Byron wouldn't shut up about Linc losing everything. One joke was okay. Linc could let it roll off his back, but after five or six snide comments, he'd had enough and clocked Byron.

The fight that ensued had cause Ma to kick Byron out and that made things even worse. Then, he'd had to hear that he was Ma's favorite over and over again.

"Ma sent me."

Bryon snorted. "Of course, Ma would send her golden boy to fetch the black sheep."

"Don't start."

"Get out. I don't need you here."

"Byron, it's mid-afternoon. Shouldn't you be at work?"

His brother worked at Linc's old plant driving a hi-lo truck. It was an easy job, but it also allowed for extra time to screw around on the clock.

"I'm at work. Just taking a break. Remember you used to do the same thing? When you didn't think you were better than everyone else? Ralph!" Byron waved the bartender over to them. "Come here."

Ralph walked over, a towel in his hand and a scowl on his face. The sixty-something-year-old man was a member of the lodge and had tended bar for years at the Elk's. The organization had been responsible for several positive community programs, which were intended to uplift the African American community in Ypsilanti. His mother had even served on the board as a member of the female auxiliary of the order.

"What's going on, Byron?" Ralph grumbled. When his gaze met Linc's, recognition lit his eyes and he smiled. "Well, if it isn't ole' Linc." He reached out and grasped Linc's hand in a strong handshake.

"What's up, Ralph? Long time."

"Too long. Where you been, man?"

"Busy." He eyed Byron out of the corner of his eye. "I'm here to take my brother home."

"Aw, shit. Why don't you stay a while? Have a beer."

Before Linc could object, Ralph pulled out a beer, and set it in front of him. Staring at the Miller beer, Linc thought about the day he'd had. His supervisor had given his machine setting job to another, less qualified white man. The Union Rep wouldn't take the case because he was friends with the man who'd taken Linc's job. To make matters worse, someone had broken into Ma's house and stolen all of her gold jewelry.

Drinking that beer would relax him. It had been a long time since he'd tasted alcohol. Could one sip really derail his progress? He sighed and picked up the bottle, gripping the bottleneck so tight he could have broken it. To his right, his brother snickered.

Visions of Layla, Courtney, and Lil Linc flashed through his mind. He'd come too far to even risk a relapse for a beer. There was a time when he thought he needed it to get through his day, but he'd done pretty well without it. His world hadn't fallen apart yet.

Slamming the bottle down on the bar, he stood and

turned to his brother. "Listen, I came here to help you. But you have to want help, bruh."

Bryon waved a dismissive hand at him. "You don't know shit about me or my life."

"I know Vivian left you. I know she cheated on you with some guy at the job."

"Well, then you know I deserve this drink." Bryon tipped his half-empty bottle of beer up at Linc. "You know you want to join me. Stop frontin' like you don't."

Ma had told Linc the entire story before he'd arrived. Bryon's wife, Viv, also worked at the plant. Recently, she'd been caught sleeping with her supervisor on the clock. News around the plant spread fast, and it didn't take long for it to get back to Byron. His brother went ballistic on the supervisor, nearly beating the man to a pulp. Fortunately for his brother, the supervisor had agreed not to press charges. Apparently, the man had a wife at home and it wouldn't have been a good look to have to go to court for getting beat up the husband of the woman he'd had an affair with.

Byron had retreated straight to the bottle and had been posted at the bar every day since he'd found out. Vivian had finally begged Ma to intervene, and Ma had recruited Linc to help.

"I won't deny it. A beer would probably taste like heaven right now. But one thing I won't do is ruin my life again."

Linc had realized his mistake as soon as he'd walked in the door. He loved his brother, but he wouldn't put his recovery in jeopardy for anyone. He didn't care if they called him soft or stuck-up or "too good for everyone."

"There you go." Byron burped and gestured toward Ralph again. "Always acting like you're better than me."

"This doesn't have anything to do with you, bruh. For once, it's about me and Layla and my kids."

When he was away, he'd written a list of ten goals that he wanted to accomplish before Christmas. All of them were important, but number one was fixing his family. He was there to get his life back, by any means necessary.

"I'll help you, bruh." Linc clasped Bryon on the shoulder. "But I can't help you in here."

Bryon balled his hands into fists and dropped his head. "Can you help this pain go away?"

Linc shook his head. "No, I can't. If I had the power to do that, I would will my own away. But I can tell you what I've done to cope with the overwhelming desire to trash myself. I can listen if you need to talk."

"Well, then... I don't need you. You can go now."

Nodding, Linc dropped a bill on the bar for Ralph. "Fine. I'll go. But you should know that drowning yourself in that bottle, won't make everything okay. It will only mask the pain until tomorrow. Then, you'll find yourself right back in this chair."

And without looking back, Linc left his brother and his beer behind.

It was only the beginning of July, but it already felt hot as hell. Layla was grateful for the working air conditioning unit at her place—and the man who'd made it happen.

She peeked through the blinds. The same man stood outside fixing the fence. He'd been working on it for a few hours. With narrowed eyes, she studied the frown lines on his face, the way he hammered the nails in the wood. He was upset about something. She'd known it the minute he'd shown up there.

Layla recalled the haunted look in his eyes when he'd stripped off his shirt and proceeded to haul the wood he'd purchased out of the garage to start on his project. She'd asked him if he was okay, but he'd shrugged her worry off. Still, she couldn't help but wonder what he was thinking, why he was wound so tight. *Or maybe I should just take his word for it that he's fine?* That would be the sensible thing to do. No sense in worrying over something that could be nothing.

Layla watched him while worked, took in the muscles in his arms to his sculpted back to his strong legs. He was magnificent in every way that counted.

For some reason, the fact that Linc hadn't broached the subject of "them" in weeks bothered her. She'd asked for it, but… *Stop it, Layla.* Shaking her head, in an effort to clear her mind, she opened the patio door and stepped outside.

"Are you hungry?" she asked.

He wiped the sweat off of his brow with his arm. "Are you cooking?"

"I had taken a few steaks out of the freezer earlier. I was going to fry them with onions."

"Steak sounds good. Why don't you let me grill them?"

"Linc, you're already doing too much."

"It's no big deal, LaLa."

Layla felt warm at his endearment. It wasn't the first time he'd called her that since he'd been home, but today it felt different. It almost felt like a declaration of sorts.

She swallowed. "It is to me."

"It's not like you haven't cooked for me before."

Layla had basically been cooking for him every night. Well, she told herself she was really cooking for her and the kids, but if he happened to be hungry, there would be extra for him. "I'm cooking, Linc. No more arguments."

"When I'm done here, do you mind if I use the shower?"

Flashes of a naked Linc in a towel—her towel—raced through her mind. She backed away, bumping into the wheelbarrow that had magically appeared behind her. Layla quickly turned her back on him. The blush that burned her cheeks would definitely be visible to him, and he'd know what she'd been thinking. "Sure. I'd better get started." She hurried back into the house.

Back inside, Layla picked up the phone and dialed Sissy.

"Hello?" Sissy answered.

"Hey." Layla pulled the steaks out of the refrigerator, then the seasonings out of the cabinet above the stove. "I was just calling to see when you planned on bringing the kids home. Did you need me to come get them?"

"I told you I'd bring them home, Layla. You know I had a kid before you graduated from middle school."

Sissy had left home right after she graduated from high school, intent on marrying her first love. It had been quite the scandal in her household back then because Sissy had defied their parents to be with Elijah. Layla's niece, Tara, was born about a year after sissy had moved out.

"I know, Sissy, but Linc is here and he wants to see the kids."

"Girl, he sees these kids every day. One day won't kill him."

Layla giggled. Linc had been adamant about tucking the kids in every night. He'd only missed a few since he'd been back in their lives. And each time he'd missed, there had been a valid, understandable excuse like work. Even when Ma had fallen off a ladder while painting the shutters and Linc had to rush the older woman to the emergency room at the nearby Saint Joseph Mercy Hospital, he'd managed to come and read Courtney a bedtime story.

"You know how Linc is, Sissy. He wants to make up for the missed time."

"And I definitely understand that. He's good that way."

Layla knew Sissy really did understand. Her sister's first marriage didn't last long. In fact, she was divorced before her second anniversary. Tara's father had never made an effort to be a father to her. But, fortunately, there were men in the family that could fill the gap. Linc had even been one of them. When Sissy had moved back from Chicago a few years ago, Linc had agreed to let Sissy and Tara stay with them.

"Yeah, he's a good man."

"Do I detect some thawing over there?"

Layla shook her head. Sissy had told her to stop being so cold to Linc and let him make amends. Reluctantly, Layla had agreed but had been adamant that there was no chance of them getting back together.

"You're not detecting anything. Bring my kids home."

"What are y'all doing?"

"I'm cooking dinner for Linc." She seasoned the steaks and cut up the onions. Linc loved her fried potatoes, and she figured it would make a good side dish. "He's been working hard on the fence out back and I wanted to make sure he ate good."

"I taught you well. And to answer your question, I'm not bringing your kids home. They're staying the night."

"What are you talking about? They don't even have a change of clothes."

"This diaper bag you packed for Lil Linc has plenty of options. And I happen to have a new outfit for Miss Court- ney. We're good here."

"Sissy, wa—"

"Bye, Layla."

The sound of a dial tone pierced her ear and Layla glanced at the phone in disbelief. *Did she just hang up on me?* Layla dialed her sister again, only to hear the busy signal on the other end. *I'm going to get her.*

Sighing, she finished preparing the meal. Once everything was ready to cook, she dropped the potatoes and onions in the pan. They'd also have sweet corn.

"LaLa, I'm done for the day. When is Sissy bringing the kids back? I wanted to see them before I left."

"She's not. They're spending the night with her. She told me the news a few minutes ago, actually."

"What do you mean she told you the news?"

Layla debated on telling him the truth because there was a lot in the conversation with her sister to unpack. Sissy had basically played matchmaker by demanding to keep the kids. Her sister wanted Layla and Linc to work things out, to get back together. It made perfect sense Sissy would behave the way she did. Still, Layla didn't have to like it.

"Long story," Layla said, with a quick wave of dismissal. "I had a box of your clothes in the basement, and I took it upstairs for you. I also set a towel and washcloth on Courtney's bed. There's a bar of soap in the shower."

"Okay. I won't take long. I pulled the charcoal out of the garage. I think grilled steaks would be good with those potatoes you're frying up."

Layla dropped a few pats of butter into the pan with the potatoes and stirred them around before placing the top on the pan. "If you insist. We can eat outside on the new table."

The other day, Linc had arrived with new patio furniture. She'd argued with him for two seconds before she'd relented. He'd given her a compelling argument filled with dinners outside and family gatherings over the summer.

"Good idea. I told you that set would come in handy."

"So what, Linc? You won. I love the new table, and I can't wait to have dinner out there."

"Thanks for admitting it. I'll be back in a few."

He disappeared around the corner. Several minutes later, she heard the shower turn on and let out a deep breath. She had half a mind to hop in her car and drive to Sissy's house to pick up her babies. Part of her wanted them there because they'd served as a buffer, a way to keep her on track with Linc. Without that safety net, she feared she'd be lost in him.

SIX

Get it together, Layla.

Layla finished with the side dishes, but her mind seemed to want to travel to Linc in the shower upstairs. She'd tried to think about the kids, burnt bread, and even communion. But all she really wanted to do was march up the stairs and sneak a peek.

Sighing, she walked to the stereo in the Family Room. She browsed the many cassettes in the box on top of the stereo. When she spotted a mixtape Linc had made for her a few years ago, she plopped it in and pressed "play."

Rufus and Chaka Khan's "Everlasting Love" blasted through the speaker and she started singing along to the lyrics. The song didn't make sense to her, but the music was nice and Chaka could sing. She swayed back and forth, hitting all the high notes.

One of her favorite things about Linc was that he was smooth on the dance floor. She recalled the feeling of being held so close to him, the smell of his cologne, and the sound of her heart hammering in time with the music as they glided to whatever song was playing.

She whirled around and let out a high-pitched screech when she saw Linc standing in front of her. With a hand on her chest, she said, "You scared me. I hate when you walk up on me like that." She swatted him playfully on his shoulder. "Did you find everything alright?"

She moved to brush past him, but he wrapped his arms around her waist and tugged her to him. Chaka Khan faded out and The O'Jays took up the charge. She wrapped her arms around his neck, and they swayed to the music.

"This song reminds me of us," she admitted.

"I hope so. I made this tape for that very reason."

Eddie Levert launched into the break and Layla couldn't help but sing along. "Your love is so good, so good, so good, so good to me."

His gaze raked over her, the heat in his eyes unmistakable. "Sing that for me again," he said, his voice low and husky.

She smirked, and did as he asked. He pulled her even closer, so close she could barely breathe. But it felt so good, she didn't want to pull away. They danced like that for several seconds before he twirled her around and brought her back to him.

With eyes locked on hers, he traced her bottom lip with his thumb. "You're so beautiful. I miss this."

Layla wanted to tell him to do something about it, but she mentally slapped her own hand. It wasn't best for her to do that. And she had to look out for herself. But, oh, she wanted it.

He lifted her palm to his lips and held it to him for a moment before brushing a tender kiss on her wrist. "I'd better put the steaks on the grill," he said.

Layla followed him in the kitchen and gathered the sides. They stepped on the patio through the Family Room door. She went to work setting the table while he prepped the grill.

It didn't take long for the steaks to cook, and before she knew it, they were seated on the cushioned chairs, stuffed from dinner. Another night when she had to force herself to concentrate on her steak and the conversation and not on how her body seemed to respond to his nearness as a moth would to a flame. The conversation went from movies to food to the kids and then back to fun times they'd had early on in their marriage.

Layla laughed. "I still can't believe you made me do that."

"You said you weren't scared." He shrugged. "It was fun."

"I hate spooky houses."

"I think you secretly loved it."

Averting her gaze, she picked at her half-eaten steak. "Maybe," she conceded. "But only because you were there."

"I hate to think of all that history, all of those memories are in the past. I know I said I wouldn't pressure you, but I still feel like we have years of good stories ahead of us."

Layla tamped down her excitement at him bringing their relationship up again. Because despite her earlier claims, life with him didn't seem so impossible right then.

"So you say," she teased.

"I went to the Elk's today," Linc admitted softly, changing the subject.

Turning to him, she watched his profile, the way he stared at the sky. Clouds had moved in fast from the west and thunder rumbled in the distance.

Swallowing, she said, "And? What were you doing there?" She didn't want to assume the worst, but the thought of him stepping foot into that place, made her want to put a halt to every amorous thought she'd had tonight.

"Ma asked me to go get Byron."

Layla held her breath, waited for him to finish. She shifted in her seat and forced her gaze up to the sky, and not at him. She wanted him to feel comfortable enough to talk to her, but she was terrified at what he might reveal.

"He was there, drinking and not giving a fuck about his life," he continued. "All because of Vivian."

Layla had heard the rumors about Vivian. It was hard not to listen to the gossip around town. Ypsilanti wasn't a small town in acreage, but it felt small sometimes because the rumor mill churned nonstop. She had first-hand experience with it.

"Well, they are married," she mused. "I can see why he'd be devastated."

"She cheated on him right under his nose."

"Women forgive men all the time for infidelity. Why is it so hard for a man to do the same?"

"You're not serious."

"How do you know that?"

"Because you'd stab me with a pair of scissors if you thought I was cheating on you."

Layla burst out in a fit of giggles. "You're so wrong for that."

"Have I said anything that's untrue?"

She shook her head. Layla considered herself a good woman, but she did have a small temper. Linc was an attractive man and she'd learned early on to not take any crap from women who thought they could approach him while she was sitting there. Not that Linc ever gave any of those women the time of day, because he didn't. Still, she wasn't against throwing a punch when warranted.

"You're not lying," she said finally.

They sat in silence for a moment, holding hands and watching the clouds darken.

"I can't go back to living without you," he whispered, so low Layla couldn't be sure she'd heard him correctly. "I need you."

His words, his simple presence, had made her feel so whole. The dance in the Family Room, dinner on the patio, the music playing through the screen door. He'd been such a gentleman, so understanding of her need for control. But he'd also remained steadfast in his pursuit of a relationship with Courtney and Lil Linc—and her.

There wasn't just a part of her that belonged to him. Everything, every piece of her, was his. She loved him more than she ever had. She wanted to trust him, she wanted to give in. But she had to be careful. Tomorrow.

She stood up, looked down at him. "Linc?"

"Yes, baby."

Layla didn't know what she wanted to say. She just knew something had to be said. Logically, she knew they weren't ready for forever yet. But her body, her mind, was ready for right now. She opened her mouth to speak, but a big fat raindrop hit her on the tip of her nose. Then, the sky opened up and drenched them both and the food in record time.

"Oh no!" she shouted.

They scrambled to pack up everything, grabbing plates, utensils, and the bowl of vegetables. He closed the grill and moved it closer to the house.

"I should probably put it in the garage."

"I think that's a good idea. I'll take the cushions."

She picked up all the cushions and dashed to the garage. He joined her seconds later with the grill. Lightning crackled and thunder boomed above them.

"I think we should make a break for it," he said.

Entwining his hands with hers, she nodded before they ran out into the rain. He picked up the stack of dishes she'd piled up on the table and she opened the door, letting him in first.

"I'm soaked." She kicked her sandals off and closed the glass part of the patio door.

He returned with a towel. "Here."

She flicked water in his face, and he returned the favor getting her in the eye. "Ugh. You get on my last nerve."

"Let me help you." He used the towel to dry her hair a bit.

"My hair is a mess."

"You're still beautiful." He brushed the tips of his fingers against her neck. The one touch sent shivers across her wet skin. Even wet, he looked downright sinful. She was almost ashamed of how her body reacted to his nearness. Almost.

"Linc," she whispered.

"Shh…" He brushed his nose against hers, and she sucked in a sharp breath.

Then his mouth was on hers, coaxing her to open for him. Which she did, willingly and finally. There was nothing gentle about this kiss, but she didn't care. She liked it. No, she *loved* it. His fingers in her hair, his tongue stroking hers, his body hard against her, drove her crazy with need. She was lost in his heartbeat.

Layla was on fire for him, burning in places that she never thought would burn again, places that she knew would never burn for anyone but him.

When he broke the kiss, he blazed a trail of wet kisses down the column of her throat. She couldn't think, not when his hands roamed her body, not when his mouth was hot on her skin.

"I promised I wouldn't come to you." He nipped her shoulder lightly, then backed away. "Remember that?"

She swallowed hard, wanting to close the distance between them again. But she remained frozen in place, eyes locked on his.

"I'm not going to make the first move. But…damn I want you."

"Linc, please."

"I told you I would never break another promise to you."

Layla sucked in a deep breath. *Oh, God is he going to leave me here, filled to the brim with desire for him?* Was he going to let her ache for him with no release?

"So, you tell me… Do you want me to break that promise? Please… Let me love you."

He inched closer, until they were nearly touching. She felt his hard erection against her stomach. It was the moment of truth. What was happening between them had been building since the moment he'd walked back into her life.

The hungry look in his eyes melted her, made her want to strip her clothes off right then and there, it was so hot. There was no mistaking the desire in his brown orbs.

Layla didn't bother hiding her emotions because she was sure he could read them on her face. Confusion, lust, fear, love, whatever. There were too many to name. But the love she felt for him, her overwhelming desire for him were the ones she wanted to hold on to at that point.

And against her better judgment, she decided to give in to his love. She didn't want to think about their past, the mistakes they'd made. She only wanted to focus on the here and now.

Without another second of hesitation, she stepped into him and pulled him down to her, kissing him deeply. It was desperate and passionate, hard and soft. It was everything she needed in that moment and not enough. She wanted more.

His hands on her body were tender, yet possessive, and she wanted to cry out. It felt so good, so right.

"Linc," she whimpered against his mouth. "I need you."

Her admission seemed to spur him into action. He lifted her off of her feet and carried her upstairs to her bedroom. Inside, he gently laid her on the bed and climbed over her, kissing her deeply and possessively.

His tongue blazed a trail to her ear, nipping on the lobe lightly before he growled, "Mine," in her ear.

"Oh, God," she breathed, unbuckling his belt and sliding it off.

"Say it," he commanded.

"I'm yours."

Slowly, he unhooked her bra. Layla felt exposed, open to his hungry eyes. He stared at her like she was his salvation. And from everything he'd shared with her, she guessed she was. The thought made her want to give him more of herself.

"Layla, please." He brushed a thumb over her nipples, before taking one into his mouth and sucking until she cried out his name. Then, he kissed his way to the other breast, paying it the same attention.

She tugged at his shirt until he sat up on his legs and pulled it over his head. Layla took a minute to let her hands roam his hard chest and abs. *Perfect*.

He nipped at her chin before taking her mouth again. He unbuttoned her jeans and dipped his hand inside her panties, sliding his fingers over her slit. His thumb circled her tiny bundle of nerves.

His name came out as a breathless whisper on her lips.

Almost like a hoarse cry. The things he did to her body made her want to beg for more.

Her orgasm hit hot and hard, rolling through her and sending sparks of pleasure to all of her nerve endings. She collapsed on the bed, chest heaving and body trembling.

A smile tugged at her lips as she burrowed into the mattress. "Linc, that was… Oh God. I almost forgot how that felt."

He chuckled and settled on top of her. He pinched her chin lightly. "There's more where that came from, baby." The evidence of his desire for her pushed against her inner thigh and she arched up to bring him closer to her core.

Leaning his forehead against hers, he gripped her thighs and slowly pushed inside of her. She gasped at the feel of him filling her up.

She wrapped her legs around his waist. He stayed like that for a moment, letting her adjust to his size. Linc had always been a generous lover. He always made sure she climaxed first.

Linc kissed her nose, before he pulled out slowly. Their lovemaking was slow initially, as they familiarized themselves with each other again. But soon the pace changed from slow and steady to fast and furious as they raced toward completion.

Layla was the first to fall over the edge, screaming his name. Linc joined her seconds later, burying his face in her neck and growling out his release.

Linc lifted his head up and smiled at her. "I've dreamed of this, Layla. I imagined the moment you'd let me make love to you."

She brushed her lips over his. "Me, too."

"Really?" He touched her nose with his, and she loved every contact, every touch. "I thought you didn't want this."

"I thought I didn't, either."

"What does this mean?" he asked, concern in his brown eyes.

Layla caressed his cheek. "It means we're still good together." He opened his mouth to speak, but she kissed him silent. "It means it's time to go to sleep. Will you stay?"

He gave her a lopsided grin. "I will."

Ruining this perfect moment with talk about the future of their relationship wasn't something Layla wanted to do. Because despite how she felt, she didn't know if she could take the risk and be with him the way he needed.

"So good," Linc murmured, dipping his tongue into Layla's heat.

"Oh, Linc," she purred.

He laved at her, his tongue circling her clit. He'd never tasted anything as sweet as her, and he wanted more. He wanted to bury himself inside her. He wanted it more than his next breath.

It didn't take long for her to come, groaning his name over and over again. Linc kissed his way up her body, biting down on her shoulder before he collapsed onto his back, pulling her with him.

They'd made love several times throughout the night and each time was better than the last. When he'd arrived the day before, he had no idea the visit would take such a turn. His intent had been to work on the fence and tuck the kids in. But fate had other plans.

"What are you thinking about?" Layla asked, tracing the lines of his stomach muscles.

"You."

She perched herself up on her elbow. "You always say that."

He tucked a strand of hair behind her ear. "Because it's true. Even when I don't want to, I think about you."

With narrowed eyes, she said, "Are you trying to run game on me?"

He laughed. "Why would I do that?"

"To get me to give in."

"But you're already here, naked in my arms. No game needed, right?"

She smacked his pec and snuggled into him. "It was the rain."

He felt her shake with a giggle and couldn't help but join her. "Keep telling yourself that."

"Linc?"

He drew invisible circles on her bare shoulder. "Yes."

"Shouldn't we have a talk?"

Linc knew Layla wouldn't be able to *not* talk about what happened between them. And he would oblige. But he worried another conversation would set them back.

"How about we get some breakfast?"

Later, Layla and Linc fixed breakfast together. He was on toast duty, while she cooked the scrambled cheese eggs and fried bologna. His favorite.

She'd admitted that she didn't start buying bologna again until last week, because of him. And he'd appreciated her honesty. Guilty gnawed at him, though. Because he hadn't told her the whole story about his trip to the bar.

"What's wrong?" she asked.

Linc stared at her. She looked absolutely stunning in one of his oversized T-shirts and nothing else. Her toes were painted a deep mahogany and her hair was piled on top of her head. He hated to have this conversation with her, but didn't want to have any secrets between them. She needed to be fully aware of his struggles. It was the only way they'd be able to make it.

"I have something to tell you," he said.

She sat back in her chair, and scooted away from him. He could practically see the armor coming back up around her. He reached out and pulled the chair back to him.

"Layla, you wanted to have a conversation, so that's what I'm doing."

Folding her arms across her chest, she nodded for him to continue.

"When I walked into the bar yesterday," he brushed his thumb over her knee, discouraged when she flinched at his touch. Sighing, he forged ahead. "I felt all types of emotions walking into a place I'd spent so much time drinking."

"What was the overwhelming emotion?" she asked.

"Sadness. Because that used to be me. Then, Ralph came over and gave me a beer." When she peered up at the ceiling, he picked up her hand and squeezed. "Can you look at me?"

She shot him a wary glance.

"I wanted to take the drink," he confessed. "But I didn't."

Layla closed her eyes, and she slumped forward. She seemed to be warring with herself over something. He gave her a minute to process what he'd said. Finally, she let out a huge breath. "Why?"

"Because I don't need it. I've spent years using alcohol and drugs to hide. I'm done hiding."

"Linc, I think it takes a lot of courage to do what you did. But I hope you don't continue to put yourself in the position to have to choose."

Linc loved his family, and it had been hard to distance himself from people who meant so much to him. His family had always made gatherings a priority, and he'd turned down invitation after invitation since he'd been home.

"I just want you to be happy," she said, lowering her gaze. She picked at a loose thread on the chair.

"I am happy, LaLa. Here with you and the kids. We could have everything we dreamed of together."

"I don't want to have it all, Linc. I never did. When we married, you promised me the world on a platter, spoiled with fine clothes, fine dining, and fine jewelry. But I didn't need those things. I just wanted you. I wanted our family."

The sincerity in her eyes would have brought him to his knees had he been standing. "We can still have our family, you know? I'm still here. It's a risk, a gamble. But what we get in the end would be worth the work."

"How do you know it would work? I mean, Linc…sex is one thing, but it's not enough to sustain a relationship. I'm not sure I'll ever fully be able to trust you. And it's not fair to put you through that, to hoist all of my baggage into the relationship. Just like it's not fair for you to expect me to carry yours. I don't want to be *that* woman. How can you build a life with someone when you're always wondering who or what they're doing? It's no way to live."

"That's the thing. We don't know if it will work. We never did. That's the risk. All I know is how I feel. I love you more today than I ever have. You've given me something no one else has. You opened your house, your life up to me again, even if you haven't fully opened your heart yet.

Layla's eyes softened. "How can you think I haven't opened my heart yet? You're here. You've been here every day practically."

"But does it matter to you? Because you said it didn't."

Linc had replayed their many conversations time and

again in his head. But only one had almost made him question what he knew about them and the love they had for each other. She'd told him she loved him but it didn't matter."

"I remember. I was angry, Linc. Hurt."

"I don't want to hurt you, Layla. I just want to love you. I asked you last night, and I'll ask again today. Please, let me love you?"

Layla caressed his cheeks and pulled him into a kiss. He swept his tongue into her mouth, reveling in the feel of her in his arms, the taste of her on his tongue. When she pulled away, she smiled. "I'm not saying that this will work, or that I won't change my mind tomorrow. But I'm willing to try."

His mouth fell open. As much as he wanted to sit her on the table and make love to her right then and there, he needed to be sure he heard her right. "You do realize what you just said."

"What did I say?" she asked, a smirk on her full lips.

"That you want to give this a try, that you want to work on us."

"Sounds like what I said. But, Linc, we need to go slow. There are some things that still need to be worked out between us and I—"

He interrupted her sentence with a hard kiss. "I get it. I understand. We can go as slow as you need."

Her hand flew up to her mouth and she blinked. "Okay. And, Linc?"

Standing, he picked her up, pleased that she immediately wrapped her legs around his waist. "Yes, baby."

"Thanks for telling me the truth. It definitely goes a long way."

SEVEN

Every year, Ma's neighborhood threw a huge Block Party. People brought food, the deejay played old and new school music and the kids ran around screaming. This year's party would be no exception. Linc was glad Layla had accepted his invitation, even though he'd noticed the clear hesitation on her face.

He couldn't blame her, either. The cul-de-sac Ma lived on was jam-packed with people laughing, playing cards, dancing, and drinking. And he knew he smelled weed. Since he'd quit smoking, he'd become extremely sensitive to the smell. Sometimes it had even made him sick to his stomach. But he'd had to come, or at least make an appearance. It was also Ma's birthday.

His mother had been bopping around with money pinned to her shirt. They had a long-standing family tradition to pin the birthday man or woman with "dollars." Depending on the size of the gathering, and the generosity of the guests, the birthday person could walk away with a hundred dollars or more.

He and Layla spent the first hour eating and yapping

with Ma. Next, they joined a game of Bid Whist against another couple. This was officially their fifth date. Over the last several weeks, he'd stepped up his game. They went to a jazz concert in the park, visited one of her sorority sisters for a game night and had dinner at a restaurant in Downtown Detroit.

Linc had followed through on his plan to take them away for a few days. He'd been off work due to a mandatory shut down, so they'd decided to leave town for a few days right in the middle of the week. The kids had enjoyed Cedar Point and SeaWorld, and Courtney had asked to go back the next day. In fact, they'd just returned last night.

The only problem was she'd yet to ask him to spend the night. They'd made love a few times since that rainy night earlier in the month, but she still kept him at a distance. It bothered him, because he wanted to be with her full-time. He wanted to go home.

Layla bumped into him with her hip, breaking into his thoughts. "Ma is so happy."

She pointed at Ma, now dancing with old Mr. Amos. He'd seen the two huddled together off to the side earlier. "I saw them when we first got here. I don't like him."

"Linc, let your mother have a life."

"It's not that, Layla. I just don't like him. He used to throw rocks at us when we were kids."

"I remember you telling me that story. I still don't believe it." She bit into a hot dog. "Why would a grown man throw rocks at innocent kids?"

"Because he's an asshole," Linc replied. "He has never been nice to me."

"If he marries your mother…"

Linc clasped a hand over Layla's mouth. "Don't finish that sentence."

Linc's parents had been divorced for years. Ma was

technically free to date, but he'd hoped his parents would wise up and get back together. Unfortunately, both of them were stubborn.

Layla laughed and pried his hand away from her mouth. "Linc, she's a grown woman with needs."

"Damn, you're going to make me sick."

"Mamas need loving every now and then."

"Are you including yourself in that?" he asked, with a wink.

She shrugged. "Maybe."

Wrapping an arm around her, he gave her a quick kiss. "You're so beautiful when your mouth is full."

Layla snorted, covering her mouth with her hands. Once she swallowed her bite, she gripped his collar in her hand. "You almost made me spit my food out."

He laughed. "I'm glad I'm not wearing your food on my clothes."

They continued to walk around the neighborhood. He greeted several people he hadn't seen in a long time. Old Mrs. Hayes still made the best pound cake outside of his Ma's house. And Mr. Fields was always telling people about the goodness of the Lord. And Mr. Booth still had a penchant for telling tall tales about his time in Vietnam during the war. The consensus was that he'd seen so many horrendous acts, he'd slowly started going insane. But everyone loved him, and still listened to him.

By dusk, the amount of people dancing and drinking had tripled. But Linc stayed close to Layla, making sure she was good.

Ma brought her a pulled pork sandwich with coleslaw and Layla dug in, moaning when she tasted the seasoned meat and Ma's special barbecue sauce. Layla hadn't had it in a long time.

Layla held her fork out for Linc to take a bite. He gave Ma a thumbs up when he sampled the food.

Ma grinned, pride in her eyes. "I made it for you, son. I knew you wanted some."

"Thanks, Ma." He took another bite from Layla's plate. "You put your foot in this."

Layla turned her back on Linc when he went to dip a clean fork into her plate. "No, get your own."

Linc's arm snaked around her waist and pulled her to him. "Baby, don't tease me. You know how I hate that." He kissed her shoulder, and trailed his tongue up to her ear. "Let's get out of here."

She craned her neck to the side and kissed him. "That's a good idea. Let me go call Sissy and check on the kids."

They'd considered bringing the kids to the party, but in the end, had decided to leave them with Sissy. The children were exhausted from their family trip. "You do that. Ma's house is open. You can use the phone in there."

She winked and planted a quick kiss on his lips. "I'll be right back."

***

Layla got all the way to Ma's house when she remembered her purse. She'd left it sitting next to Linc, and she needed it. Turning on her heels, she rushed back to the party. She scanned the crowd, looking for Linc.

Off to the side, she saw him, chatting with Rod—the same man that had been at the drug house with him, the same man that had just handed Linc a bottle of gin. Fear paralyzed her to the spot. No matter the progress, no matter the desire to live a clean and sober life, he still had to live with the temptation to go back to that old life. There would always be a part of him that wanted the high that drugs or alcohol could give.

And now the question for her was, *Can I trust him*?

Things had been great between them over the last several weeks. Every day, they'd grown closer, shared more of themselves. But a part of her still hesitated whether to let all of her guard down. And staring at the irrefutable truth in front of her, she knew why. Despite his best intentions, he really could succumb to his addictions again. Where would that leave her? Where would that leave Courtney and Linc?

She dropped her head when he looked up, praying he didn't see her. Confronting him seemed too drastic and walking away seemed too weak. Instead, she chose to stay and watch for a minute, to see what he'd do when faced with his drink of choice—"the bumpy face," as they called Seagram's Gin.

"What are you doing here, baby?"

Layla jumped, whirling around to face Ma. "Um, I—well, I was just—" she stuttered.

Ma peeked over her shoulder and frowned. "That asshole," she grumbled. "I can't stand him. I'm going over there to break that shit up."

Layla gripped Ma's wrist. "No, don't."

"Linc shouldn't be anywhere near nasty-ass Rod," Ma argued, a frown on her face. The older woman looked downright murderous, and Layla couldn't blame her. She wanted to kick Rod's ass herself.

"I know, Ma. But Linc is a grown man. He's going to encounter these things often. We have to let him be a man."

And even though Layla had said the words, she was terrified that Linc would take a sip out of that bottle.

"I know you're right, but that's my son. I already have

one son ready to throw himself into the Detroit River over a no-good, hoe-ass woman. I can't afford to lose Linc. He's doing so good."

Linc was a great man. He'd done so well since returning home, and Layla would hate to see him relapse. Having him around had become comfortable again. He'd already done so much at the house, he'd devoted his time and energy to the kids. One day soon, he'd be able to quit his job at the plant to open his own business.

She glanced at him over her shoulder, noticing the strained look on his face. He and Rod seemed to be in an intense conversation, and it almost looked like Rod was yelling at him. And that damn bottle of gin was still in Linc's hands.

Put it down, baby. Give it back to him.

"Oh, Lord," Ma whispered beside her.

It almost felt like they were watching a side show, waiting on the one-eyed gorilla to come out. They watched the scene unfold with rapt attention.

Layla let out a sigh of relief when Linc shoved the bottle back in Rod's hands. The other man wasn't too happy because he pointed angrily at Linc. At that point, Linc snatched the bottle away and threw it on the ground, shattering it into tiny pieces. Then, she watched Linc walk away from the other man, shaking his head and wringing his hands the entire way. He disappeared behind the house on the corner.

Ma went to follow him, but Layla stopped her. "He's okay, Ma. He just needs some time."

She hadn't thought when she'd assured Ma, but she knew it was the truth. Linc would never have taken that drink, even if he wanted to. The realization that she actually believed that was sobering, and told her everything she needed to know about herself. It was time for Linc to come home.

Back at Ma's, Layla paused when she saw Byron sitting on the porch, a drink in his hand and a scowl on his face.

"Wow, sis. I haven't seen you in a month of Sundays. What brings you here? Wait, let me guess. My dear brother."

Layla eyed her former brother-in-law. They'd always had a good relationship before the divorce, but lately he'd been a jerk to her. She'd only seen him a handful of times since Linc came home and each time he'd been rude and snide.

Sighing, she said, "Byron. How are you?"

"Wondering why my brother is so damn gone over you," he sneered.

Layla attempted to walk past him, but he grabbed her arm. Furious, she yanked her arm away from him. "Don't *touch* me, Byron!"

"What is it about you?" He stood and picked up a strand of her hair. "You're fine, but you're not worth him leaving us behind."

She pushed him away. "You're drunk, Byron. Why don't you go somewhere and sleep it off?"

"I'd rather not. Did you know Viv cheated on me?"

Layla scanned the area, hoping someone would come along to interrupt this conversation.

"Did you hear me?" Byron sipped his beer and blew in her face. "I'm talking to you."

"I'm leaving." She turned to leave and tripped over a beer can, right into the arms of Linc. When she met his eyes, she felt scared for Byron. Linc looked ready to pummel his brother.

Linc steadied her. "Are you okay?"

She nodded. "I just tripped."

He spent a few minutes checking her over, brushing his thumbs over her face and neck. "I've got you." But he wasn't looking at her. His gaze was fixed at a spot over her shoulder.

"Linc." She wrapped her arms around his waist, hoping her presence would diffuse his anger.

He removed her arms. "Give me a minute, baby."

Before she could answer him, he gently pushed her aside, grabbed Byron by the lapels of his shirt, and lifted him off his feet. "What the hell is your problem?"

Byron struggled, squirming to get loose from Linc's grasp. "Let me go, bruh."

"Brother or not, keep your hands to yourself. If you ever, in your life, put your hands on my wife again, I will fuck you up. Believe that."

Layla tried hard not to swoon at the way Linc had come to her rescue. And she couldn't help the surge of pride that coursed through her at the way he'd called her his "wife." No, they weren't married anymore, but the fact that he still thought of her as his wife made her heart soar.

"I just told her like it is," Bryon said. "She's the reason the family isn't together anymore. We were fine until she came into the picture. Now you're acting like you're too good to hang with us anymore. You can't even chill with your family and have a beer."

Linc slammed Byron against the screen door. "Man, shut the hell up. Layla isn't the reason I nearly lost my life getting high. That was on me. And your behavior is on you. Either way, that's no excuse for talking to her like you're crazy or putting your hands on her. I meant what I said. Touch her again and you won't like my reaction."

Linc dropped Byron and his brother tumbled backward and fell on his butt. Byron jumped up and lunged for Linc. Layla screamed as fists started flying. The fight bled out into the grass, but not before they crushed Ma's flowers.

Byron was bigger than Linc, more husky. But Linc was stronger, and sober. It didn't take long for Linc to overpower Byron. Linc landed an uppercut to Byron's jaw, knocking him to his back. "Get up," Linc hollered. "Get your ass up."

Layla rushed over to him and tried to pull him back, but he wouldn't budge. "Linc, please. Don't do this. He's drunk."

"He's pathetic," Linc countered.

Byron scrambled to his feet. "Man, what is your problem? You're going to beat me? I'm your brother."

"I told you," Linc spat. "I love you, but I can't help you when you're like this. You may think it's no big deal to have a drink or smoke a cigarette or even a joint, but I can't go there again. I don't want that life anymore, man. My life is with Layla and my kids. And if you can't respect that or her, then we have nothing to talk about."

"She left you." Byron glared at her. "She divorced your ass, and changed her last name."

Linc glanced at her. "I left her first."

Tears welled in Layla's eyes. She'd said the same thing to him weeks ago, when they'd finally ripped the Band-aid off of old wounds. He'd heard her. He understood. That simple knowledge made her love him even more.

"I left her the minute I started lying, cheating, and stealing to get high."

"Whatever, bruh." Byron spit into the flower bed. "I don't have time to hear that goody two-shoes bullshit."

Linc raised his hands up at his sides. "And I don't have time for you, if that's how you're going to be."

"Maybe if you'd—"

The front door opened then, and Shante stepped out

on the porch. Her eyes were wide and wet with fear. "Uncle Linc, Auntie LaLa, there's something wrong with Lil Linc. Sissy is on the phone."

Layla cried as Linc sped toward St. Joseph Mercy Hospital. It was one of the largest hospital networks in Michigan and a short drive from Sissy's house. According to her sister, Lil Linc had a fever, and she'd given him Children's Tylenol like she'd done for her own children many times.

The Tylenol didn't help, so she'd walked in the bathroom to run an alcohol bath for him. When she came back out, Lil Linc had turned blue. Panicked, she'd rushed over to him and the baby lost consciousness.

When Layla had talked to Sissy, her sister had been hysterical, sobbing so loud Layla had to hand the phone to Linc. Her heart couldn't take it if something happened to her baby. And she'd been, what? Having fun, getting into it with Byron and thinking about everything else but her babies.

Linc placed his hand on top of hers. "It's going to be okay, baby. We're going to get through this."

"What if…?"

"Don't say it." His voice was strong, sure. "He's going to be fine."

Layla looked out the window, and prayed for a miracle. They made it to the hospital in record time, and Linc dropped her off in front of the Emergency Room so he could park. She rushed inside and was immediately ushered to the back.

When she entered the hospital room, Sissy was rocking Lil Linc in her arms, singing an old church song their mother used to sing to them years ago. Without thinking, Layla joined in, harmonizing with her sister. She walked toward them and picked Lil Linc up.

He was so hot, so still. But his eyes were open. She sent up a silent prayer for healing and kissed her baby's brow. "My baby. Mommy's here." She rocked her son.

A few minutes later, Linc joined them in the room. He walked over to them, brushed his hand over Lil Linc's brow and kissed their son's forehead. "Love you, son."

Layla watched Linc love on his son. Many fathers their age refused to show love toward their sons, making the excuse that it wasn't manly. But she loved that Linc wasn't afraid to tell Lil Linc that he loved him, or even give him a kiss.

Linc looked to Sissy and gave her a hug. "Thank you for acting so quickly. Has the doctor been in yet?"

Sissy explained how the paramedics rushed them there, and Lil Linc regained consciousness sometime during the ride. One of the paramedics seemed to think he'd experienced a febrile seizure, and had asked if he'd had a fever for a prolonged period of time or if she'd known of any infections.

"They took a blood sample and urine test," Sissy continued, running a hand through her hair. "The doctor should be in shortly."

Dr. Paul Monroe entered the room as if on cue. Layla held her son while he examined Lil Linc. The doctor basically reiterated what Sissy had told them, but also added that febrile seizures don't usually have lasting effects and that he expected Lil Linc to be "good as new" in a few days.

Once the doctor left, Layla sobbed with relief. She felt Linc's hand on her back, sweeping up and down, giving her his strength. While the doctor had been in the room, Linc had taken control, asking all the important questions. For once, she could focus on her son because she knew Linc would take the lead with the hospital staff.

"I told you he would be okay," Linc said, sitting next to her and wrapping his arms around her and Lil Linc. "Our boy is strong."

She smiled. "He is. Just like his daddy."

Linc cupped her cheek with his hand. "And his mommy."

Leaning into his hand, she said, "I'm glad you're here. I don't know what I would have done without you."

"Hopefully, you'll never have to find out."

"I love you, Linc."

His eyes raked over her, almost as if he was trying to see the truth in them. "I love you, too."

Linc opened the door and held it open for Layla. She walked in holding Lil Linc in her arms. They'd spent five hours at the hospital. The doctors had run every single test they could and the news was good. Lil Linc had a febrile seizure. According to the emergency room doctor, febrile seizures were usually triggered by fever in young children. It didn't appear to be related to an underlying condition, so they'd given him an antibiotic and sent them on their way.

He eased his son from Layla and walked him upstairs. She followed close behind. Quietly, they readied him for bed. Once he was settled in, they stared down at him.

"I can't stop staring at him," Layla said.

Wrapping an arm around her shoulder, he brushed his lips over her temple. "That's normal. We had a big scare."

She sucked in a deep breath. "I don't think I've ever been that scared before. I love him so much."

Linc knew how Layla felt. Before they had Courtney, he couldn't fathom the love between a parent and child. It was different than his love for Layla. Being a father was a privilege. He had the opportunity to sow positive seeds into someone's life, from birth to adulthood and beyond. He wanted to leave them a legacy, one that mattered.

"You're such a good mother."

She glanced at him. "Thank you. I appreciate you saying that."

"I know it hasn't always been easy, but you handle motherhood with grace. Even with all you've been through, you still manage to engage the kids, to love them unconditionally." Linc hated that he had caused of most of her struggles, but he was glad he'd been there to hold her up during this time. "I couldn't have asked for a better mother to my children."

Entwining her fingers with his, she squeezed. "He's sleeping. I sure could use a cup of coffee."

The change in subject wasn't lost on him, but he decided not the overthink it. Following her to the kitchen, he pulled down two mugs from the cabinet while she made the coffee. Once she finished, she brought the two mugs over to the table. It felt like Déjà vu. Not too long ago, they'd sat at the same table and had the hard conversation. But they'd survived it, and he thought they'd come out stronger for it.

"Something on your mind?" he asked when she didn't speak for what felt like an eternity. "You're very quiet." She twisted her mug around on the table, and he got the feeling she was purposefully avoiding eye contact with him. So, he prepared himself for bad news.

"Can you stay tonight?"

His eyes widened. He didn't know what he'd expected her to say, but that wasn't it. Going back to his apartment that night had been a foregone conclusion. "I can stay."

"Can you stay forever?" she muttered under her breath.

Linc blinked, unsure he'd heard her right. "What?"

She looked up then, her eyes shimmering with unshed tears. "I realized something tonight. Well, today, when I saw you turn away that bottle of gin Rod offered."

Linc frowned. "You were there?" He had no idea she'd seen the scene between him and his former best friend.

The argument had cemented the end of their friendship, and he couldn't say he was hurt. He'd known for a long time that Rod wasn't the friend he portrayed himself to be. Linc had cut Rod some slack time and time again because they'd been friends since middle school. But it was way past time to sever all ties. The fact that Rod had brought a bottle of gin to the block party to celebrate Linc's return from rehab had been a dead giveaway that Rod didn't want better for himself, or for Linc.

"I saw him hand you the bottle. I saw you argue with him. I saw you give the bottle back. Then, I saw you throw it to the ground."

"Why didn't you say anything?"

"Because you needed to deal with Rod on your own, Linc. And because I finally realized that I trusted you to not take that drink. I won't lie, I was scared. But more than that, I was confident. My faith in you was justified."

Linc could hardly believe the turn this night had taken. He'd gone into today hopeful that she'd finally ask him to stay the night. What he'd gotten was better. She trusted him, even though he'd hurt her, even though he'd forever be a recovering addict.

"It got me to thinking. I know we're divorced. I know this seems sudden, but…" She stood and walked over to the junk drawer. Opening it, she pulled something out and made her way back to the table. "I forgive you. I've watched you work hard to maintain your sobriety, even when I'm sure you weren't even confident in yourself.

You've kept every single promise you made to me and the kids—and more. When I've needed you, you made yourself available to me. You made me cubed steak with gravy. You knew I needed to have control of this situation and you backed off until I was ready to come to you."

She held out her hand and he slid his into hers. Standing, he pulled her into his arms and hugged her. They stood like that for a moment, enjoying the nearness of one another.

Finally, Layla pulled back. "I'm so hopelessly in love with you. And I don't want to go another night without you lying next to me in our bed." She placed a key in his open palm. "So, come home.

"Layla." He searched her eyes. "Are you sure?"

She grinned up at him. "So sure. I don't want to dwell on the past anymore. I'm done waiting for the other shoe to drop, because what if it doesn't? Then, I would have been sitting here letting life pass me by."

Linc stroked her cheek with his thumb. "You don't know how much this means to me."

"I think I do, because it means the world to me. Baby, we're still us. I still love you more than all the stars in the sky. You still set my heart on fire with one glance. And you are *still* the one I want to spend my life with."

He pressed his lips to hers, pulled her closer to him. "Thank you for believing in me. I love you, baby. And I'm coming home. For good."

"Good. Now, take me to bed."

EPILOGUE

Five months later

"It's beautiful." Layla stared at the round-cut diamond on her ring finger. "You always know what I like."

Linc kissed her bare shoulder. "I know you. That's all that matters."

She smiled, remembering all that had happened over the last few months. He had moved in the day after they'd brought Lil Linc home from the hospital. The kids had been ecstatic to have him in the house full-time, and so was she. They'd slipped back into their routine easily, which made her happy.

Then, when the school year started, Layla had decided to cut back on several activities in order to spend more time with the family. But when she'd written her letter of resignation as the Union Chair, Linc had ripped it to shreds and told her "to give them hell."

She guessed his reaction had a lot to do with his job at the plant. He'd had more bad days than good there, but his college classes had helped to break up the monotony. He'd be a college graduate in less than two years, and Layla couldn't be more proud.

He'd arrived home earlier that evening and told her that he'd arranged for Ma to keep the kids so they go could on a date. Dinner had been at Mountain Jacks in Ann Arbor, Michigan. Linc had pulled out all the stops, telling her they had reason to celebrate. It was December, and snow had been falling for hours, but he wouldn't cancel their reservation. He'd insisted on braving the elements.

When they'd arrived, the maître de had shown them to a secluded table near the back of the restaurant. He'd ordered for her, which always gave her a thrill because he knew her so well.

Layla recalled how the waiter came to the table and set a wine menu and a box in front of her. Then, right there in front of everyone, Linc had dropped to his knees and asked her to marry him—again.

From there, dinner went a little something like this— eat, kiss, drink, touch, laugh, kiss. By the time dessert arrived, Linc asked the waiter to box it up and practically dragged her outside. It had taken less than twenty minutes to make it home to their kid-less house, and Layla couldn't have been more thrilled.

Linc's voice pulled her out of her trip down memory lane. "LaLa?" He tapped her shoulder.

She blinked. "Huh?"

Layla was lying on her back, sated from the oral treat he'd just given her. Her new dress was a tattered mess around her waist. He'd been frustrated when it had taken a minute too long to unbutton her dress, and ripped it off.

He slid the remains of the torn fabric off and rested on top of her. "Your attention should be on me, not the ring."

Grinning, she wrapped her arms around his neck. "I'm sorry. I just love my new ring."

When she'd opened it earlier, Linc had told her it represented a promise—a promise to hold her forever, a promise to be there forever, and a promise to love her for the rest of their lives.

"I love it, too. But I need your eyes here." He pointed at his own eyes.

Dipping his head down, he took one nipple in his mouth. She held his face to her and reveled in the feel of his tongue against her skin. He gripped her hips, digging his fingers into her skin. Then, he slowly entered her.

Pleasure washed over and through her as he moved, slowly at first. He took his time, making sure she felt every inch of him. He'd filled her so completely, she could barely catch her breath.

Layla was consumed by him, branded by his love. She knew it wouldn't take long for her to fall over the edge. When his pace picked up, she was right with him, meeting him thrust for delicious thrust. She felt her orgasm build in her, in her bones in her belly, in her limbs and her mind. Kissing him deeply, she dug her fingernails into his scalp, loving his low groan of approval.

He broke the kiss. "Tell me how much you love me. Tell me how I'm the only man you need forever."

Layla couldn't respond if she wanted to, because she was too busy coming. Her orgasm stole her breath, wrung her dry. Soon, he followed her into bliss.

Once their breathing evened out, she hugged him to her, not willing to let him go even for a minute. "I love you so much, Linc. There will never be anyone for me but you. And I can't wait to be Mrs. Wilson again."

She'd told him that before, but she would never grow tired of telling him what he meant to her.

He looked at her then, his eyes filled with emotion.

"You've made me so happy. I was made to love you, to hold you. And I'm ready for forever with you."

Layla kissed him on the chin. "Forever, it is."

THE END

DEAR READER,

Exploring the complexities of love in the 1980s has been an amazing experience. Being part of the Decades project, working with so many amazing writers, has been a huge honor. I'm so grateful to that I was able to share Layla and Lincoln's story with you.

Writing Made to Hold You has been a rewarding experience, one that has allowed me to grow as a writer. This isn't simple a second chance at love story, it is a story of redemption or rising above our circumstances and being better. When I embarked on this journey, I made it my mission to give readers a happy ending for a couple devastated by drug addiction.

Layla and Lincoln are near and dear to my heart. Their story gave me all the feels. It is love unconditionally and against all odds. It is choosing to forgive and move forward. It is the best of black love.

I hope you enjoy the journey!

Love,

Elle

www.ellewright.com

As the new editor-in-chief for LA Chronicle, Traci Johnson is determined to change the California paper's narrative. She's tired of stories

about police brutality, gang violence and drugs, and wants to focus on positive African-American stories. But when rapper Tupac Shakur gets shot it's breaking news that must be covered, even though the incident epitomizes the type of topic she's trying to avoid, and the type of man she despises.

Marcus Moore is a product of South Central Los Angeles. He could have easily been one of its statistics but he stays out of trouble and becomes an undercover agent for the LAPD. When Tupac gets shot he knows it's not random. In fact he believes the trail of blood will lead back to a group of men he's investigating, the reason he's in Vegas. Meeting sexy journalist Traci Johnson is a tempting distraction, but her assumptions based on his appearance and the culture he embraces are a huge turn-off.

Tupac dies, and Marcus surprisingly finds comfort in Traci's arms. Will what happens in Vegas stay in Vegas, or can the two get past stark societal differences and turn one night's passion into a lifetime of love?

DECADES:
A JOURNEY OF AFRICAN AMERICAN ROMANCE

January — February — March

DELICATE AFFAIR — LINDSAY EVANS

Secret Desire

LOVE'S SERENADE — SHERYL LISTER

April — May — June

ART OF LOVE — SUZETTE D. HARRISON

LOVE'S SWEET Melody — KIANNA ALEXANDER

PRIDE & PASSION — CARLA BUCHANAN

July — August — September

PROMISE ME A DREAM — WAYNE JORDAN

ELECTION Day — KEITH THOMAS WALKER

MADE TO HOLD YOU — ELLE WRIGHT

October — November — December

THUG Love — ZURI DAY

INCONSEQUENTIAL CONSEQUENCES — DENISE JEFFRIES

CAMPAIGN FOR HER Heart — PATRICIA SARGEANT

ONCE UPON A BRIDESMAID SERIES

When four bridesmaids come together to support their best friend's wedding, they realize that most of the people they know have already tied the knot. Whether unlucky in love or single by choice, these besties make a pact to change their relationship status. The goal is simple… Each woman has one year to find Mr. Right and say 'I do'. Between passionate one-night-stands and best friend hookups, these bridesmaids are in for a wild ride. Are they in over their heads? Or will one impulsive wedding pact change their lives… forever?

*** Beyond Forever excerpt on the next page***

Yours Forever by Sherelle Green (Book 1)
Beyond Forever by Elle Wright (Book 2)
Embracing Forever by Sheryl Lister (Book 3)
Hopelessly Forever by Angela Seals (Book 4)

EXCERPT: BEYOND FOREVER

ONCE UPON A BRIDESMAID, BOOK TWO

The Pact

Wedding schedule, wedding colors, wedding programs, wedding pictures, wedding toast number 5,789, wedding blah, wedding shit... If Ryleigh Fields heard the "W" word one more time, she was liable to choke someone—namely her BFF Ava Prescott for putting her in this situation in the first place.

It wasn't like she wouldn't walk on hot, molten rocks with her bare feet for Ava. She would do that and more for her besties, Ava, Mackenzie Cannon, Raven Holloway, and Quinn Jacobs. It wasn't even that she'd been forced to wear a two-hundred-plus-dollar chiffon, floor-length dress that she'd never wear again. In fact, she was pretty sure the dress would be in the trash before she left the reception hall. *Who wears pewter anything?* No. It was simple. Weddings made everyone go bat-shit crazy. Like abso-fuckin'-lutely insane.

Ryleigh was over-the-moon happy for her friend, Ava. Really. She'd even admit to shedding a tear when the happy couple exchanged those heartfelt, handwritten vows. But between the wedding planner sending multiple emails a day and barking orders about folding programs and walking in a straight line, Mrs. Prescott nitpicking about centerpieces and menu choices, and Ava crying at the drop of a hat about Lord knows what, Ryleigh was fed up. She mistakenly thought she was home free after the ceremony, but the wedding planner from hell still wouldn't leave her alone. And she hoped—no, she seriously prayed—that she could get out of town without going the fuck off on the next person that asked her when she was going to be next. Because this shit was getting on her fucking nerves.

Ryleigh turned her attention to her friend Quinn, who was standing before them with a smile as wide as that damn fat cat in Cinderella. Ryleigh wanted to make an excuse to leave because Quinn had been waxing poetic since Ava announced her engagement months ago, and she just wasn't in the mood for fairy tales. Her life was anything but, and one man with a cute smile and a magic penis wouldn't change her mind. Sure, she knew Q was the hopeless, poetic romantic in their crew. She didn't begrudge that because that optimism had gotten her through the worst times of her life. But damn... She was tired and pretty sure her hair looked a hot mess because of all the manual labor she'd been forced to do. She was so sick of this freaking wedding.

Sighing, Ryleigh rolled her eyes and twisted in her chair to face Mac and Raven. "Can we just tell her to shut up now?" she mumbled under her breath. "The wedding is over, and my drink is gone. Ouch." Ryleigh rubbed her leg where Raven had pinched her.

Despite the sting that radiated in the spot, she couldn't help but smile at Raven. She'd missed them. These women weren't just her friends, they were her family. The only family she had. Growing up in the tight-knit community of Rosewood Heights, South Carolina had presented many challenges for Ryleigh. The town was too tiny for her taste, especially since she'd been the black sheep of their group of friends. Always the charity case, Ryleigh had come to hate their small-as-hell town. The whispers about her crazy mother and absent father hadn't abated in the eleven years since she'd left for college in Michigan. She'd endured the sympathetic smiles of the old church ladies who pretended to want to help her but gossiped about behind her back. The kids on the playground had teased her mercilessly about her lack of fashionable clothes, but she'd dealt with it. Ryleigh had known early on that Rosewood Heights was not her endgame and she worked damn hard to be self-sufficient enough to make sure she'd never have to darken her mother's doorstep, begging to come home, like Harriet Fields swore she would.

"Ha!" Mac's voice brought her out of her reluctant trip down Rosewood Heights Memory Lane starring every-thing-that-was-wrong-with-this-damn-town. "Anyone within a thirty-mile radius can hear her squeal when she starts talking about love and shit."

Ryleigh didn't know what had transpired before that point, but she could agree with Mac's statement. She gave Mac a high-five. "Girl, you can say that again."

"If everyone's done making fun of me, can we please continue this discussion?" Quinn said, clearing her throat.

Shit. Ryleigh scanned the area for anyone that she could convince to bring her another margarita—with a double shot of Patron preferably.

Kicking off the four-inch strappy sandals Ava required they rock, she slouched back in the wicker chair.

Raven leaned over to her. "Don't look now, but you have an admirer."

"If it's not Idris, I don't care. Where is that damn waiter?"

As if on cue, the young waiter appeared before her with fresh drinks. *Yes*. She snatched her top-shelf margarita off the tray, winking at the cutie pie. *Too bad he's one foot out of jail bait*.

"I think we should toast." Quinn held up a shaky glass full of margarita that Ryleigh knew she wasn't going to finish. *I'll finish that one, too*. "Here's to us all finding that special one and saying 'I do' this time next year."

What the…? Slamming her glass down on the table, Ryleigh resisted the urge to bolt. "Oh hell no."

She vaguely heard Raven say something next to her, then Mac, but she couldn't recall what it was because she was too busy wondering what the hell was wrong with Quinn. They all knew she was itching to follow in Ava's footsteps down the aisle, but how did that equate to all of them trotting their asses to the altar, too.

Quinn continued, but Ryleigh had effectively blocked her out. No way. No fucking way. She was going home. It was time to get off this train before it was too late. She turned to Raven, who'd apparently lost her damn mind, too, because she was raising her glass in agreement. Then, she looked up at Quinn. It was the hopeful look in Q's eyes that did her in every single time. And her hopeful friend had just issued a "Best Friend's Challenge." And she'd never backed down from one, in all their years of friendship. No matter how crazy they were. And this was crazy as hell. She wasn't even dating, or trying to be anyone's girlfriend. She had plans for her life; ones that didn't involve becoming a wife.

Okay, so she could agree to this right now and then not get married. Simple. It wasn't like there was money or a promotion on the line. They weren't in a damn Lifetime movie. After a year, she wouldn't be married, and that was all to it. Losing the challenge wouldn't be the end of the world. She was grown ass woman. She'd lost before, sometimes on purpose.

What could they do anyway? Fire her from being their best friend because she didn't find and marry some man in one year. *Who does that anyway*? Shit, Ava and Owen had been dating for years before he'd proposed. It was a harmless, hopeful toast that would make her friend feel better. She could do that.

Slowly, she raised her glass as Mac and Quinn went back and forth about something.

Finally, Mac raised her glass and Quinn said, "To finding that special one and saying 'I do' by this time next year."

The four friends clinked their glasses, and Ryleigh gulped down the rest of her drink. It wasn't nearly enough to get the sour taste of that toast out of her head. With that in mind, and without another word, she stood and made a beeline for the bar.

WELLSPRING SERIES

Unimaginable luxury. Longstanding wealth. A powerful family empire that controls the town of Wellspring, Michigan. But three heirs are done—with all of it. Now one by one, these very different siblings are seizing control of their lives . . . and daring to find real hometown love.

Touched By You excerpt on next page

Touched By You (Book 1)
Enticed By You (Book 2)
Pleasured By You (Book 3)

EXCERPT: TOUCHED BY YOU

WELLSPRING SERIES, BOOK ONE

Chapter 1

The ground was wet. Cold.

But Carter Marshall couldn't bring himself to move, to walk away. He clutched the weathered copper ornament in his hands. It was the only thing he had left of his old life, the only tangible reminder that they both existed. Everything else was gone, charred beyond repair.

"I'm not sure how to do this,," he mumbled to himself. He knew he had to let the anger go now. It had consumed him, filled him to capacity and pushed him to keep going. He wondered what would take its place, or if he'd even be able to let go of the hate he had in his heart for the man who had taken away everything.

The rain pounded on his head, drizzled down his face. It had been an hour since he'd arrived, but he couldn't bring himself to complete his task. Instead, he'd sat there, his expensive Tom Ford suit soaked and his Cole Haan shoes muddy. Nothing mattered anymore. Not his wealth, not his name, not his work. Everything that he'd once held dear seemed like a curse now.

"I'm sorry," he muttered. "I'm sorry I wasn't there. I was too obsessed with work, too driven, too focused on my damn money. I thought if I just worked hard enough, I could give you the life you deserved. I only wanted to make you happy."

His eyes welled with fresh tears. As if he hadn't cried enough already. The loss of his beautiful wife and daughter had devastated him to his core, weakened him. Even now, almost two years later, he could still smell the gasoline, taste the smoke in the air, hear the screams of the neighbors as the fire burned. He recalled the determination on the firemen's faces as they worked to put the blaze out, and he remembered the exact moment they all realized that it was too late.

You're the best part of my day, my hero.

Her words still haunted him. *Her hero*. His wife of three years, his college sweetheart, had told him he was her hero. Only he didn't feel heroic. What was the opposite of hero? Coward. Loser. Nobody.

Instead of being home with his wife and newborn daughter, he'd been working. Late. It seemed his work had eclipsed everything in his life, despite his denials. Krys had told him time and time again to live a little, to enjoy life. But the lure of the prestige, the money, the connections that his business guaranteed was important to him. He'd worked too hard, too long to let it go. He'd been distracted, meetings all day and projects to finish. When the phone rang, he'd moved it to voicemail with a little text that said Give me a minute.

To think that was the last thing Krys heard from him . . . He'd been so busy he couldn't even pick up the phone and answer. Was she scared? According to the arson investigators, the fire had started around seven o'clock. The call from her came through a little after seven. What if that one phone call could have changed something? Countless hours in therapy, numerous assurances that he couldn't have known, did nothing to quell the guilt he felt every time he looked at her response to his text. The worse part was that he hadn't even seen her response until hours later, after he'd been ushered from the scene of the crime. It read, I love you. Always remember.

Even in her last minutes, she'd been thinking of him. And he'd been thinking of his next project, his next dollar. *What good is all the money in the world without her, without them?*

Closing his eyes, he willed himself to move, to do what he came to do.

He scanned the area around him. It was *their* spot. Krys had insisted they visit as often as possible since it was the place where he'd proposed.

Today would have been their wedding anniversary. Remembering her beautiful face on the day he made her his wife made his heart ache. Krys was beautiful, in a classic "Clair Huxtable" kind of way. She was a good woman, believed that taking care of the home, being a wife and mother was the best job in the world. They'd been so young, so full of hope.

People had questioned him about the choice to marry so soon after college graduation, for even being with the same woman for so long. Even his best friend and business partner, Martin Sullivan, had been wary. And he'd known Krys for as long as he'd known Martin. Carter couldn't explain it, though. He wasn't an impulsive person. Every-thing Carter had done in life had been carefully planned. It was the reason he and Martin had been so successful. Neither of them played around when it came to business.

Marrying Krys, though, was his destiny. At least, he'd

thought so at the time. She'd supported him through some of the worst times of his life—the death of his youngest sister and his grandmother and his parents' subsequent divorce. Krys never wavered, never wanted him to be anybody but himself. She'd never complained when he traveled for work or forgot to take the trash out. She was perfect, and he didn't deserve her. He'd broken the promise to love and to cherish, to have her and to honor her. If he had, he would have answered her call. He should have been there. Especially since she'd always been there for him. Krys had given him the best gift he could ever have— her heart, her body, her soul. He'd promised to protect her, to be there for her. *Except I wasn't, not when she needed me the most.*

Time hadn't made this wound better, hadn't healed him like they told him it would. He'd started to resent them —his parents, his friends, his employees . . . everyone. The questions were becoming unbearable. The sad looks infuriated him. Most of all, when people told him *It will be okay*, he wanted to slap them. Because he was not okay, and wasn't sure he would ever be okay again. He knew he had to try, though. For them. For Krys and for his baby girl, Chloe.

Carter closed his eyes and inhaled the wet, night air. It was too late to be the father Chloe needed. She wasn't even a year old. He'd never heard her say "Da Da" or had the pleasure of watching her toddle into his waiting arms for the first time. *It's not fair.*

The tears fell freely down his cheeks and his stomach lurched into his chest. *I failed.* Carte looked down at the gold Christmas ornament in his hand. It was a glass heart, personalized with their names, their wedding date, and some of their favorite things. Krys had purchased it for their first Christmas as a married couple. Sighing heavily,

Carter dropped the ornament into the small hole he'd dug, next to the tree where he'd dropped on one knee and proposed to his first love, his only love.

"I made them pay, Krys."

Within days after the fire, the Detroit Police Department had arrested the young men that were responsible. But pressure from city officials had them backtracking on the investigation. Of course they did, because one of the men, the main culprit, was the son of college-aged one of the most influential business owners in the city.

The McKnight family was well-known in the Detroit area. Carter had effectively launched a smear campaign, blasted them on every social media site. Through his own computer skills and those of his partner, they'd crippled the McKnight business. Revenge was best served with a depleted bank account. A guilty verdict wasn't enough for him. He'd just been awarded a settlement in the civil lawsuit he'd brought against the city and the family for hampering the investigation.

Money wasn't his motive, though. He wanted them to lose everything, just like he had. Those men had destroyed his life on a whim, because of a bet. They'd targeted his house because it was on the corner lot in a mostly African American neighborhood—because they could.

"I donated most of the money to the burn unit at Children's Hospital and set up a foundation to help burn victims and families who've lost everything to a fire."

It would never bring them back. He knew that, and he'd certainly paid the price of the personal vendetta he'd waged against the family and the city, with his family and his work. The criminal and civil trials had taken a lot out of him. Now, it was time for him to let the anger go, let them go. That was the hard part.

He covered the glass ornament with mud and stood to

his full height. By all rights, he should be celebrating. He'd won. His mother had set up a family dinner, and his brothers had mentioned a hookup he had no intention of taking advantage of. What would be the purpose? Sex? Because that's all it would be. He was empty, a void that would never be filled.

"Everyone wants me to move on, but how? Is it even okay to love someone else?"

And now he was officially crazy, talking to the night air, to Krys like she could actually answer. At the same time, if he had a sign, maybe he could let go fully. His wife and child died, but his love never would. That much was certain. *I don't have room for anyone else.*

"I love you. Take care of each other."

Sighing, he made his way back to his car and, after one last glance at the tree, sped off.

A houseful of people awaited him when he arrived at his mother's place about an hour later. There were old friends, cousins, and more cousins. The smell of fried chicken wafted to his nose, and his stomach growled.

"Carter, get your butt in here."

Iris Johnston was a loud, formidable woman. She pulled him into her strong arms and squeezed tightly. Carter wasn't an overemotional person, rarely gave out hugs, but he couldn't help but wrap his arms around her plump waist and relax into her embrace.

"Ma, I thought it was only going to be family." He pulled back and kissed his mother on her cheek. "You promised not to make a big deal about this."

Iris shrugged and gestured to the table of food in the corner. "Eat. You deserve this. You've had a tough few years."

His stepfather, Chris, joined them and patted him on

the shoulder. "She's right, Carter. Have a seat and relax yourself. This is the least we could do for you."

Carter walked through the house, greeting the people who'd turned out for him. One by one, they hugged him, gave him sad glances before they offered more congrats and condolences. *Shit*. It was like Krys and Chloe had just died. His thoughts flashed back to all the food his mother insisted be dropped off to the house, all the stares.

When he finally made it to the kitchen, he grinned at the sight of his brothers.

"Carter, I'm glad you're finally here," Kendall said, giving him a quick man-hug. "Mom has been worrying the shit out of us." Kendall was the baby brother, and officially a college graduate as of two months ago. It had been a happy day when he'd walked across the stage, because they all thought he wouldn't make it.

"Yeah, man. She was a nightmare." His brother, Marvin, leaned against the sink. Carter reached out and clasped his hand in their signature handshake. Marvin was the middle son, the lawyer of the family.

"Well, I'm here. Not sure how much longer, though. I told her I didn't want a party."

"Baby brother, if you leave, we're all going to have to pay for it." Carter turned to see his older sister, Aisha, standing behind him. "And let me tell you, I'm sick of y'all fools leaving me behind to clean up your messes."

Carter pulled his sister into a tight hug. "I'm sorry, sis. But you know crowds are not my thing. I'm getting antsy just listening to the chatter."

Aisha's expression softened, her brown eyes wide with unshed tears. "I know. But you have to start living again. You know Krys would want that." She rubbed his cheek. "You can't die with her. You're still here for a reason."

Carter blinked and prayed for an intervention, anything to stop the pain in his sister's eyes. She was worried about him. Being the oldest of five siblings, Aisha had been a sponge her whole life, taking on their emotions like they were her own.

"I don't want to talk about this," Carter said, leaning down and kissing his sister on the forehead. "Where's the food?"

Aisha's shoulders fell, and she nodded. "I'll fix you a plate."

Moments later, he was sitting at the small table in the kitchen, eating while the party roared on in the other room. Aisha sat across from him, watching him eat.

"I've been calling you. When are you going to come back to the office?" she asked. Aisha worked as the chief financial officer of Marshall and Sullivan Software Consulting Inc. She basically kept the company up and running while he and Martin traveled the world. His sister had been calling him for weeks, every single day. "Martin needs you back in the office."

Carter knew he'd been a lousy business partner. Martin had basically picked up all the slack in the last two years. It wasn't right for him to continue this way. And with his best friend recently tying the knot, Carter wanted to be able to step up again to let him be a happy newlywed. "I know, Aisha. I plan to go back soon."

"Soon? The office has been inundated with calls, requests for proposals. You're on the verge of something bigger than you ever dreamed, especially with the Wellspring offer. Don't give it all up."

"Aisha, please shut up!" he snapped. His sister's mouth closed in a tight line, and he immediately regretted his outburst. "I'm sorry. It's just . . ." *Forget it.* She wouldn't understand. Work was the last thing he wanted to do, because work was what he'd allowed to get between him and his wife for too long.

"I get it," his sister said, picking at the table with her thumbnail. "You're hurting, and I don't want to take that away from you."

He was such an asshole. Aisha had only been trying to help, to take care of him like she'd always done. It wasn't her fault he was incapable of being social. He had never really been the type of person that enjoyed being around a lot of people. Carter had always been more solitary, preferring to be by himself than go to the club.

"I didn't mean to yell." He dropped his fork on his plate. "But Krys is gone, Aisha. She's fuckin' dead, and so is my baby girl. It takes a huge effort for me to get out of the damn bed in the morning. I just . . . I need some time."

"I know Krys is gone, Booch. I get it."

Carter groaned at the use of his childhood nickname. Only a few people still used it, but it always reminded him of being a kid. He wasn't a child anymore. He wasn't going to conform to everyone's ideas on how he should handle his grief. Shit, he was the one that had to go home every night to an empty house, an empty life.

"No, you don't get it, Aisha." Carter pushed away from the table and stood, pacing the floor. "Please stop pretending you do." He pointed at his chest and whirled around to face her. "I'm the one that has to deal with the fact that some ignorant prick decided to set fire to my freakin' house. With *my* family inside. I'm the one that has to look at myself in the mirror every day, knowing that my wife was scared and needed someone to talk to her and I didn't answer the phone."

"You can't be everywhere at once, Booch. You were working. Krys understood that about you."

"How do you know what Krys understood?" The

anger that rose up in him was irrational and directed solely at the one person who didn't deserve it. "She needed me." Bile rushed up his throat and he fought to control it from coming out, spewing over his mother's hardwood floor.

Aisha stood and approached him, fire in her brown eyes. She gripped his chin and twisted it downward to meet her gaze. "You want to know how I know? Krys called me."

Carter's eyes widened. "What?"

"I didn't want to tell you because I knew it wouldn't help you at the time. You had the trial and then the lawsuit. It was keeping you going. Now that it's over, I need you to hear me, Carter."

He swallowed roughly, clenched his hands into fists.

She sighed. "Krys called me that night. She knew she wasn't going to make it." His sister's eyes filled with tears. "She needed to talk about some things. One thing she made sure she said was that she loved you. Carter, she loved you. Everything about you. But she knew you. She knew that you'd let her death consume you, she knew you'd let this ruin you. Your wife, my sister-in-law, wanted to be sure that you didn't. She wanted you to live, to have a life even though she wasn't here. She made me promise to tell you when the time was right. I'm telling you now."

Exhausted and emotional, Carter gave in, letting the tears that had filled his eyes spill. He fell back into the chair. His head bowed, he whispered, "I don't know how to do this, Aisha. How can I live without her?"

Aisha pulled a chair in front of him and sat down, tilting her head to meet his gaze. "It won't be easy. But you have to. You deserve to live. That's what she wanted for you. God didn't keep you here so that you can die a slow death, in your grief."

"What else did she say?" His voice cracked. "Was she scared?"

Shaking her head, his sister squeezed is knee. "Krys cried, but not because she was scared for herself. She was in a bit of a panic because she didn't want Chloe, your baby girl, to suffer. She was scared for you, for the family she'd leave behind. I, on the other hand, was hysterical with the tears."

Knowing that Krys wasn't scared for herself didn't surprise Carter. His wife was never scared. It was something he'd always loved about her. During labor, she'd refused to take pain meds. But she'd squeezed the shit out of his hand. So bad, he'd needed it iced afterward. "I can imagine you bawling. You're such a big baby."

"Hey, I'm still the oldest."

The room descended into silence as they sat there. Finally, he said, "I miss her." The admission was probably obvious to his sister, but it was the first time he'd said it out loud to anyone. It was like he'd been walking in a haze, refusing to show anyone that he was affected. Only the people closest to him could tell, and that was because they knew his routine, his personality. Everything about him had changed that October night.

Aisha pulled him into a strong hug. "I know."

They stayed like that for what felt like an eternity, him being held by his big sister. They'd grown up, but remained close. As children, they were joined at the hip. Only two years apart, Aisha had dragged him everywhere with her, to all the parties. She'd been taking care of him since they were toddlers, when she would sneak him cookies under the kitchen table.

When he pulled away, he brushed her tears away. "Thank you," he mouthed.

She gave him a wobbly smile. "Always."

"What's going on at work?"

"So much. Martin is handling everything, but I don't want him to get burned out. He's finally settled with Ryleigh and they're happy. They deserve some time to just be newlyweds. Traveling to Wellspring, Michigan, is not ideal for him right now."

Carter thought about Aisha's plea. She was definitely right. Martin did deserve to enjoy his new marriage. And he had to step up and let him.

"Who was scheduled to go with Martin to Wellspring?" Carter was so out of touch he couldn't even remember the Wellspring project particulars.

"Walt." Walter Hunt was the new software engineer they'd hired a few months ago. "He's not strong enough to handle point on this project. Handling a project of this magnitude is too much for him."

Carter rolled his eyes. Parker Wells Sr., president of Wellspring Water Corporation, had hired Marshall and Sullivan because they were the best in the state, and they'd designed an excellent Enterprise Resource Planning system. And his sister was a big part of that. *Aisha is right. This is too big a job to trust to anyone other than me or Martin.*

"So what are you going to do?" Aisha asked, a mixture of worry and challenge lining her face. "Someone is supposed to be in Wellspring on Monday to meet with the players. We've pushed the date back already. If we don't do this—"

"Calm down, Aisha." Carter had the perfect solution—one that would give him time and space from the emotions that surrounded him in Detroit. "I'll go. I'll head the project myself. And I'll leave in the morning."

Carter and Aisha talked for several more minutes, working out the details of his trip. Aisha also gave him updates on a few other issues with the company. He would leave first thing in the morning and drive to Wellspring, which was approximately a three-hour drive from Detroit. A hotel had already been booked for Martin, so Aisha was charged with switching the reservations to Carter's name.

"Aisha?"

His sister turned toward the door. "Hey, girl!" Aisha stood and hugged the woman who'd interrupted their conversation. "Long time, no see. Carter, remember Ayanna? We went to high school together."

Carter smiled at the woman. He definitely remembered Ayanna. The woman standing before him, with her light skin and light eyes, was still as beautiful as he remembered. Instead of the trademark braids she'd rocked in high school, her hair was wavy and flowing down her back. But the attraction he once had to her was long gone.

Ayanna was also his "first." And judging by the way Aisha was singing her friend's praises, his sister didn't know. There were rules, after all. Back then, Aisha had banned him from ogling her friends. Little did she know or even realize, her friends weren't exactly shy when it came to him. Carter might have been a one-woman man when he met Krys, but he hadn't always been that way.

Aisha was yapping away, catching up with her friend. And Ayanna was checking him out. The heat in her eyes told him exactly what she was thinking.

"How have you been, Carter?" Ayanna asked, batting her long lashes. "You've been in my prayers."

"I'm good. And you?"

"I've been enjoying life." Ayanna inched closer to him and wrapped her arms around him in a tight hug.

Carter inhaled Ayanna's scent. She still smelled the same. It would be so easy to take it to the next level. The look in the woman's eyes when she pulled back and shot him a sexy grin was an invitation. Any other man would have run with it. All Carter felt was cold. But this could be what he needed to move on. He just wasn't sure he believed that.

"I didn't know you were coming," he said, wondering if Ayanna was the "hookup" his brothers had told him about. Only Marvin knew of their dalliance all those years ago.

Ayanna folded her arms over her breasts. "I actually was in the neighborhood, saw the cars and decided to stop. Your mother sent me in here to give you my best wishes."

Aisha piped up. "You should totally stay. There is plenty of food, and we'll be playing cards later. It'll be good to catch up."

"I'd love to," Ayanna said. "It's a shame that we grew up together and barely see each other."

Detroit was a large city, with a population of almost seven hundred thousand people. Plenty of the people he'd grown up with still lived in the city, but seemed so far away. Many of the kids he went to school with had left, though. Some had moved to the suburbs, and others had left Michigan altogether.

Growing up in Detroit was a good experience for Carter. His parents both worked good jobs, and their neighborhood was a safe haven for him. Everyone knew each other and looked out for each other. He remembered block parties and going to the skating rink with friends. No matter what the outside world thought of his city, it was his home. Although he'd had plenty of offers from different companies, he'd never considered moving. It helped that Krys was also from Detroit. They'd actually grown up fifteen miles away from each other, but had never met.

Thinking of Krys brought him back from the walk down memory lane. Even if Ayanna was giving him "the eye," he had no business even considering it. Especially today.

Taking a deep breath, Carter grabbed his still-full plate and tossed it in the waste bin. "I'm going to go out and talk to Mom before I leave," he announced to the two women. "I'll call you in the morning, Aisha—before I leave."

Even if he hadn't believed it was a good idea before, he was sure that taking on this project was the perfect solution —a new town, a new opportunity where no one knew him. Wellspring might be the welcome change of pace he needed.

ALSO BY ELLE WRIGHT

Edge of Scandal Series

The Forbidden Man

His All Night

Her Kind of Man

All He Wants for Christmas

Once Upon a Bridesmaid Series

Beyond Forever

Jacksons of Ann Arbor

It's Always Been You

Wherever You Are

Wellspring Series

Touched By You

Enticed By You

Pleasured By You

ABOUT THE AUTHOR

There was never a time when Elle Wright wasn't about to start a book, wasn't already deep in a book—or had just finished one. She grew up believing in the importance of reading, and became a lover of all things romance when her mother gave her her first romance novel. She lives in Michigan.

Join the Elle Wright Reader Group!

Connect with Elle!
www.ellewright.com
info@ellewright.com

www.ingramcontent.com/pod-product-compliance
Lightning Source LLC
Chambersburg PA
CBHW051955170626
46808CB00007B/2624